MAGGIE H

MAGGIE HEMINGWAY was born in Orford, Suffolk. After an early childhood spent in New Zealand she returned to England and worked for some years in publishing before becoming a full-time writer. Her novel THE BRIDGE won the Royal Society of Literature's Winifred Holtby Prize and was made into a film. EYES is her fourth novel and follows STOPHOUSE BLUES and THE POSTMEN'S HOUSE.

Maggie Hemingway died in 1993.

Maggie Hemingway

EYES

**British Library Cataloguing in
Publication Data**

Hemingway, Maggie
  Eyes. – New ed
  I. Title
  823.914 [F]

ISBN 0–340–59913–8

10 9 8 7 6 5 4 3 2 1

Printed and bound in Great Britain
for Hodder and Stoughton Paper-
backs, a division of Hodder Headline
PLC, 338 Euston Road London NW1
3BH by Cox & Wyman Ltd, Reading,
Berks.

EYES

From the silent reed-fringed bay of the lagoon the water presses back across the flat land, through cuts and channels. Past tilled earth and fields of maize dried by the September sun and vineyards already stripped of their fruit. The pulse of water getting thinner and thinner. No more than a trickle. And then a drop, lying in the ditch at the gates of La Pianta.

At La Pianta, beyond the cascading fountains of water nymphs, the carriageway winds back towards the house past low clipped hedges and parterres, past groups of cypress and stands of feathery trees. By these devices the facade of the house is almost entirely hidden from the road. It stares out over the terraced garden, over the soft unfurling of spring, the buzzing heat of summer. It stared out then at the beginnings of autumn, at leaves already tinged with yellow and the high, clear sky softening into pale gold with the hastening of the afternoon.

The knot of men, who stood with their horses on the gravel sweep below the portico waiting for their young kinsman, shifted their weight uneasily from foot to foot. They glanced at the massive doors, the rows of windows along the facade, and at each other. And we, concealing ourselves with practised art behind those apparently blank windows, watched them.

Inside the house the marble treads of the grand staircase rising up from the dim cavernousness of the entrance hall gleam with an almost silk-like softness – some property inherent in the marble, some trick of the light from the pair of oval windows set unusually low.

To the stranger they appear always treacherous, those stairs, slippery as smoothed and rounded ice. At their foot the red and black and white tiled floor offers no security, no firm territory. Instead, by the placing of the lozenge-shaped tiles one against the other, the floor seems to leap up at you in rusted red and black mantraps, boxes which will close round your foot like a vice.

Up in the picture gallery a door opened and closed. You had to be quick of hearing to catch it; the doors in La Pianta close more quietly than in any other house in the Veneto, the wood beeswaxed to a buttery softness, the locks oiled to silence. The Duke orders it so. But the secretariat is located only the width of a passage and an interconnecting room away from the picture gallery. It is quite simple to leave the doors ajar without suspicion. To keep the head bent to the papers on your desk and then, when the tread of the august footsteps are past, to lift it. In safety. To incline it and concentrate the hearing. In such a household as this where all is secrecy, it is no more than a matter of prudence to equip yourself with as much knowledge as possible.

The audience was clearly over. Men's voices moved in murmuring snatches of sound close to the stairs. A figure appeared, then another, at their head. His Grace and the young emissary.

'Come,' repeated the Duke, 'we'll go downstairs together!'

The young man at his side drew back, just for a second. Fleetingly, he steadied himself with the tips of his fingers against the vast bronze at the head of the stairs. And just as swiftly the Duke shot out his hand, taking the young man's arm in his bony fingers, lifting it sharply from the Neptune's flank. Federico could never bear to have anyone touch his things. Never. Not even, it was said, as a boy. Not without his permission, his invitation. Even then there was an unwillingness in that invitation that made the boldest falter. His skates, his hoop, his wooden soldiers were all possessed by him with a cold ferocity. The desire to touch, in such situations, evaporates, the eager hand draws back, but – with the invitation out you could not draw back; there he'd be watching you out of those small, dark, round eyes, tensed and lithe. La Lucertola. The lizard. It became his nickname and it stuck. The touch and scrabble of a lizard's claws over your skin at first disgusts; alarms. Until you become accustomed to it. The young man stiffened in Federico's grip, but he could not pull away. Could not refuse this favour from the Duke, this – familiarity. For Federico was laughing now at his ear, all joviality to cover the business over the statue. His thin lips slid back over his long jaw in a swiftly flashing smile – lizards smile, have you not seen it? and snakes too until that long, thin, black, deadly tongue comes flickering out. The young man's feet seemed to bump from step to step of the stair. If Federico had not been holding him he would, perhaps, have fallen. No doubt it felt to him as though the Duke's digging fingers were not there in camaraderie or for support and that at any moment – at the next step of the stairs – would come that quick, covert push. But all at once the fingers lifted from the young man's arm and the marble floor at last spread out firm beneath his feet. There were the great panelled doors and a servant waiting in the shadows to open them. But the Duke had halted and drawn his fur-edged robe closer across his chest. Federico always felt the cold more keenly than other men.

'My most earnest greetings to your master. Tell him I'll send Tomaso here with the papers tomorrow and authority for all arrangements. Tell him his generosity and my longing make further delay unnecessary. And to the Lady Emilia . . .' the Duke paused significantly and the young man swiftly bent his head to give such favour its full obeisance, to indicate the honour the Duke did his house '. . . my life-long devotion.'

Then, while the young man's head was still bent, there was a rustle and the quickly dying whisper of soft leather

5

against marble, and when he looked up it was, instead, into the small peevish eyes of the Duke's Secretary. He could not turn to see where the Duke had gone, he could not show on his face his anger at being forestalled before he could deliver his own speech of farewell. Federico never could resist these small displays of power, his prerogative of insult.

'Until tomorrow, Messer Bernardo,' said Tomaso in his low clear voice that was as soft and sinuous as a drop of mercury running away over the floor. And as they inclined their heads stiffly towards one another the heavy doors were pulled back on their hinges, there was a rush of cool air and the echo of birdsong and patterned sunlight darted suddenly across the chequered floor.

The black raven of La Pianta we call Tomaso. Black rat would be more like, he slips so silent and with such speed through all the maze of this great house, his small dark eye everywhere, seeing everything.

Back up the stairs he came. His shadow fell across our doorway, but all heads were bent; and then was gone again. Eyes lifted from under lowered brows, watching him. Like a rat to its hole, he did not even pause outside the Duke's study, the door left ajar for him.

Federico did not look up as his secretary slipped through the half-open door. He went on staring into the fire, tapping the index finger of his right hand lightly against the arm of his chair.

'Gambugliano,' he murmured, rolling the word on his tongue, drawing it out to savour the pleasure of it. Gambugliano lay to the north of his land, from the boundaries of the village of San Eustachio up onto the wooded slopes of Monte Leone; there was a sawmill, and over a dozen outlying farms, all in that black, volcanic earth that could crop twice a year.

From the door Tomaso watched the firelight flicker over his master's face.

'Megliadino,' he prompted and watched the quick

tremor of the Duke's lips at the thought of its vineyards and close clustered hamlets. 'Granze,' he added swiftly and saw at last the beginnings of a smile tighten along the thin, snout-like jaw.

'Granze, Tomaso, Granze – is there not also some manufactory at Granze? Eh?'

'A quarry,' replied Tomaso coming forward. 'One of the largest in the area, the quarry of San Pietro e Paulo.'

But Federico was already nodding as though he'd known the answer all along, his eyes half-closed, the smile still on his lips.

'Who would have thought, Tomaso,' he murmured 'that the old man's lands would be quite so extensive? He settles half on her already.'

'He cannot hope to match the honour of your blood, sir, so he . . .' Tomaso bent down to add another log to the fire.

'You go tomorrow morning?'

'I thought perhaps early afternoon.'

The Duke nodded. 'Take some toy; the usual thing, a kitten or a basketful of doves. And come to me in my study before you go and I'll give you some trinket or other.' Federico turned back to the fire, biting his lip. 'He seems to leave himself only Malo – unless he has more than we know of.'

'She *is* his only daughter, sir.'

From Malo, perched on its little hill, you can see out over the flat plains of the Veneto almost to the sea on a clear day. Behind it and to either side rise the steep wooded slopes of the Euganian Hills. They push straight up out of the level plain like a child's drawing – like the representation of mountains on an ancient map. In the mists of autumn and the fogs of winter they seem to float above that white, silent sea, islands again.

The day that Tomaso rode to Malo there was no mist, it was clear and bright. It was an easy ride alongside still canals, past fields of maize stubble and low-trellised vines. As the hills grew closer and taller so the earth under his horse's hooves grew blacker; at first in traces only, here and there, then in patches, a kind of streaking and marbling, the colour darkening until the grey crumbly loam was black and soft. This was the fabled soil for which the farmers of the Veneto felt such sullen envy, into which they cut their criss-crossing ditches and channels, not simply to irrigate their dry fields, but to carry away, grain by grain, in floods and heavy rains this black gold.

Any journey outside the walls of La Pianta was a pleasure to Tomaso. With a page at his side and two men-at-arms behind, the servant becomes master. But Tomaso was careful, was watchful, even in his pleasures. Tomaso did not forget himself like other men, in drink, or talk, or the spontaneous delight of the moment. By his order his attendants rode in silence at strictly maintained distances from Tomaso's horse. Yet who could bring proof that such a thing was not to uphold the reputation of the Duke's household abroad, but solely to flatter the pride of his Secretary? He rode apart from them, staring straight ahead, neither acknowledging the respect of the peasants that they passed, nor the whirring up under their horses' hooves of partridges. He had a habit of holding both reins unnaturally high off his horse's neck in his right hand, so that his hand minced and swayed in the air with the movement – they had the copy of it to the life in the stable-yard and kitchens – and should his horse have bolted he would have found himself in the nearest ditch. The full velvet cloak that was flung back over his right arm and draped close over the left was double-lined; the shirt, that some might say was too loosely laced at his neck, was of the finest white lawn; and his breeches were pleated and slashed in the French manner, black on black – all was black. Tomaso had never been seen in anything but sober, workaday black, and so how could the slightest charge of peacock vanity, of presumption above his station, stick? And who would dare try it? Tomaso was careful, and any man who underestimated that watchful caution was a fool.

As the plain ended and the first slopes of the hills rose around them, Malo lifted itself slowly, a smudge of ochre in all that green, until they could make out its pink tiled roofs, its crenellated tower and the black spear-points of cypresses that wound away behind the house out of sight.

Tomaso turned to the page riding at his flank.

'You have your words?'

Filippo nodded.

'And the cat?'

The boy touched a finger to the lidded wicker basket tied to his saddle and a new outburst of mewing started up.

To get to Malo you could not approach it straight, there was no pathway up its steep hill on that side. You must ride round the base of the hill and from the other side make your assault. Where the carriageway started stood tall iron gates scrolled with leaf-work and the barbs of arrows. But they hung always open.' Grass grew at their side and they were twined about with weed and convolvulus; the gravel was unraked and mixed with earth. On one hand a line of cypress climbed the path with you and yet were held, motionless, in their own shadow. All the rest was buzzing sunlight and grass burnt by the heat and roses sprawling in ropes of blossom, run wild.

There was, so we heard, a silence to the place that afternoon, an emptiness, as if they were not expected. They slowed their horses, hanging back as the house was reached, all except Tomaso, who rode forward, head up like a pointer scenting the air. Nothing could hide itself for long from him. And there was indeed the sense of something hidden, they all felt it; a jagged stillness, like time shocked into immobility in the aftermath of some violent event. Some reverberation of it echoed away over the lawn and the low wall beyond; tumbled down the hill and lost itself before you could catch it among the dense trees that clothed all the close-surrounding hills. Each

9

man looked up at the house and almost expected to see the last few grains of masonry roll from a wall that had just collapsed. Or to hear the final slithering splinter of crockery smash on a tiled kitchen floor. They reined in their horses and stood uncertainly in front of the pitted marble colonnades above which crumbling stone stairs led in a double curve to a long, arched balcony. And though, a second later, servants ran out to take their horses' heads, it was a second too late. A second full, to Tomaso, of implication. Of insult.

He climbed the wide stone steps up to the balcony and glimpsed a dark shadow fleetingly behind Count Treviso's effusive welcome. And another in the quickly lowered eyes of the footman, who offered them wine from a silver tray, and the maid, who snatched at his cloak and riding gloves and darted away again.

'Bring your glass,' said the Count, 'we'll go into my study.'

'I have with me,' Tomaso motioned Filippo to come forward, 'another emissary. One from the heart of Duke Federico, who begs an audience with the Lady Emilia.'

There was a momentary silence. The Count half-turned like a sleepwalker with a fumbled gesture to the servant who waited at the door. His smile now hung on his face like a cobweb and a blankness glazed his eyes. Yet so slight, so slight, Filippo later confessed to feeling only surprise that the old man should appear – confused – by such a request. But Tomaso, Tomaso would pounce on such an awkwardness, so that you could almost hear the leap of his thought, the seizing of his quarry. At the soft whisper of skirts in the doorway, he turned as swiftly as the Count. He did not miss the glance that passed between Count Treviso and the tall woman in the plain brown dress who then came into the room. Or the quick nod of her head. Or the low, urgent question which seemed to ignore the presence of strangers.

'Emilia?'

10

'Donna Emilia' – the woman's eyes were cold as stones picked out of the bed of a river – 'is in the garden.'

Behind his back, Tomaso's fingers twisted jerkily, lacing in and out of each other. The audience with the girl was a spectacle he had thought, mistakenly, to have little significance. But if he took the basket from Filippo now, the boy would stumble, would look lost. Tomaso's purpose would not be well-achieved. To everything Tomaso did there was a purpose – a purpose of his own.

If Tomaso might have been prevented from seeing how Donna Emilia took Duke Federico's suit, then, by chance, Lodio and Bernardo, standing on the gravelled space before the house with the horses, saw it all.

Where the afternoon sun could catch it, there had been placed an arbour with a stone seat. And towards this they caught sight of a small procession making its way over the grass: a young girl, with three of her women. Donna Emilia. She sat down on the bench and the women fussed around her spreading out her skirts and primping at her hair. Little more than a child tricked out in pink rosebuds and a new satin dress, a sulky child with long slender fingers and a perfectly traced mouth and eyes so dark they made her skin look white as swans' feathers.

They saw Filippo led out to her. He stopped in front of the arbour and bowed. Though it was too far away for them to hear, they could tell he had begun his speech, for they saw the women bite their lips and smile. But not the girl, not Donna Emilia. They saw Filippo sink to one knee and hold out the basket. Saw the small hands in the folds of pink satin twitch, an infinitesimal movement, the fingers like opposing claws attacking each other, the knuckles white for a second. The light wind lifted the ribbons on the basket and let them fall again. The women looked uncertainly at each other. One of them touched their mistress on the shoulder with the tip of a finger, covertly so that the page should not see. But she did not move. They saw Filippo's arms tremble and then steady. Finally he laid the basket on the ground, took two paces backwards and bowed deeply. The basket lurched and then toppled over. The women burst out laughing, turning to each other, bending one by one over their mistress. Lodio and Bernardo could almost hear the lilt and fall of their exhortations. At a sign from the woman in brown, one of them went forward and untied the long ribbons. She lifted from the basket a small white kitten. Amidst a fluttering of hands and a cooing of delight it was placed on Donna Emilia's lap. The kitten scrabbled for a hold on the slippery material, then Donna Emilia suddenly seized it and leapt to her feet. As she swung it high in the air and it hung limp from her hands, they saw the dark stain widening on her skirt. They saw her throw back her head and laugh, a loud cascading laugh and then, with a countrywoman's unsentimentality, hurl the animal from her. As it sailed through the air the light flashed on the gold of the coral and pearl-studded bracelet around its neck. But Donna Emilia, without another glance, was already striding back over the lawn towards the house.

Lodio and Bernardo stared at each other and then, so they said later, glanced up at the house to see who else had seen the girl. And there, in the corner of one of the windows, they had caught sight of the familiar black figure of Tomaso, watching; staring down as if he could not draw his eyes away.

On this part of the coast the dunes pile themselves high
against the sea all the way up to La Chapelle in the
north and as far south as Sanjou; troughs and ramparts
of sand threaded and laced together with marram grass.
The moaning buzz of the wind rises and falls, then rises
again so high, so sharp that it sings at the ear. Sand
singing all the length of Belle Plage, singing till it
deafens you. Finest, softest sand on the Picardy coast:
trickle it through your fingers and it's soft as silk, stand
in the path of it when the wind teases it to a fury and
it'll cut you to ribbons. It trickles between the gnarled
roots where the matted grass can't hold it. Always shifting, always moving. Your boots sink in the soft gullies
as you climb. You stagger and lurch and the sand slithers
round you holding you tighter, holding you fast. Like
quicksand. Fragments of shell fall with it: black ringed
mussel shells and the broken fans of *coquilles de roses*.

At the top of the dunes the grass lays itself flat under
the bluster of wind. Turns itself white, all its dark stalks
willowy as reeds in a stream. The dunes drop quickly,
steep, down into the marsh. Down onto land lying lower
than the shore. Land sunk. Lying quiet under still water.
Bleeding at every gash, at the mouth of every channel,
rust red. At the edges of pools. In the mud around the
thin rivulets that bubble up and dribble away again
among the reeds. Ochre-red. Blood-red. And in some
parts, leaching out into the reddened puddles, overlaying
them, twisting in tendrils and filaments, snaking out
over their surface – lies the blue. Not the blue of speed-

13

wells or the sky. Or eyes. Yet it has a way of looking
back at you, that blue; of arresting you. With its brightness, its boldness; with the unnatural shine of it as it
lies there in specks and trails. Like poison lying in the
blood. Like a water snake, coiled against the body of its
victim. Not inches away swans sail the slow-winding
cuts. And the level water breaks with the swimming
ripples of eels passing. But neither fish nor fowl will go
where it lies. And Leon, even after all these years of
walking the marsh day in day out, will not come upon
such places without a scolding cry, a low muttering of
rage and sharp indrawing of breath. He will not have it
smear the stout marsh pole he carries, nor slip against
the sole of his boot. As though its touch would burn
instantly. As though its sharp contagion could bite
through leather and cloth to strike at his heart.

Tracts of reed and long shallow pools. Warm almost.
Silent. Save for the fidgeting cries of waterfowl and the
whispering of reed flags bending all together under the
wind. Nine kilometres north to south, wound in and out
with paths. Narrow, mud-banked causeways above the
seeping water, thin trails of trodden-down reed that loop
and curl and double back upon themselves among the
floating islands of sedge. Eighty-nine hectares and all
the reed thereon. Eighty-nine hectares all to our charge,
one dwelling house and sundry outbuildings. And the
francs prompt on the table in the notary's office up in
Epay every quarter day, without fail: Michaelmas,
Christmas, Lady Day and Midsummer Day. Year after
year. Clean shirt and clean stock and no speck of mud
on the dubbined boots. The money hot in your pocket
and the boots all dust by the time you get to the outskirts
of Epay, your feet, used to the featherbed of reed, jarred
by the hard walking. And Leon, wild flowers in his
hands, lagging behind, always one step behind, eyes full
of the strange, dry inland countryside.

From Pont St Honore you can see the sand dunes rising
like mountains, silhouetted black all along the skyline.

You can smell the sea. You can feel the freshness of the sea wind whetted sharp like a knife against the salt air. But up there they've turned themselves away from it. And the marsh, too. Not a fisherman left among them now. Drainage is all their talk. And farming. Marsh turned to cornfield.

Beyond Sanjou the landlord's draining. An engineer brought from Paris and machineries dragged into quake by horses wild with panic when they feel the ground slip and suck at their hooves. Horses lamed and men injured and engines sunk in the mire. Reed grubbed up and the water led away and the rich mud left bare to crack and dry. We walked down one day, other side of Sanjou, to see the work. A dead sight it was. All the way home through the shoulder-high reeds, on the narrow familiar paths with the *pik-pik* of coot all around us Leon beat his palms together, slapping one hand against the other and sliding it off again, as though trying to rid them of a dirty mark, now and again his head jerking as though it were twitched on a rope. Couldn't eat his supper, but threw it cold to the dog and sat outside in the twilight knitting his brows and shaking his head and every so often putting up his hands to his ears to keep out some tumult. Silent.

Never spoke, Leon. Never spoke from birth. Never spoke in his life, only a gargled cry. Only a gasp in the throat. A repertoire of noise – and what else is speech? – a whole assortment of breathings and gurglings. There were none of us that couldn't follow him, even as a baby, what it was he wanted to tell us. He could communicate by the expressions that flitted in and out of his eyes alone, never mind all the passions that passed across his small mobile face, quick and changeable as March clouds. He was regarded as a thing of wonder rather than pity. When he learned to add movements of his body and all manner of shapes and signs with his hands to his repertoire, he became the entertainer of the family. What other men learn as theatrical tricks, my brother devised by himself as a natural means of expression. His was a dumb show that had our mother helpless with laughter, or her face twisted with pride, as out of his chubby hands flew all the birds of the marsh and from his hoarse throat came all their cries. Our father would take him up on his knee each evening when he came in from reeding. 'Well, my little Pantagruel!' That's what he would call him – my little Pantagruel – 'Well, and what have you done today?' And the performance would begin. The small body would twist and turn in its story and then wriggle to be put down, when he would caper over the floor, hands and eyes and face working, describing every step of his little adventures. Why he did not speak, no-one could fathom. He knew the words. Indeed he would not proceed from stage to stage of his narrative, he would not rest content, until we had guessed aloud each part of his story. We told him back his tale, who or what he had seen, and then his face would light up and he would nod vigorously as though at muddleheaded pupils who with only a little more application could be quick and sprite-sharp as he.

They put him to my charge: it was the way, the elder learning the younger. And he became my shadow. Save for the times he'd slip away alone. We soon learned not to fret for him, to leave him be and not holler over the marsh after him. The marsh was home to him, another home, with creatures in it that accepted him as wholly as did we. His marsh lore came natural and quick to him. He could smell quake, sense a false path that would lead into lying water. My brother trod so silent through the reed that, alongside his slow boots, the moorhen would pick her way between the tall stalks quite unconcerned, long-toed and delicate-stepping. And the heron, fishing in some deep-hidden cut, would stand mirrored and post-like, with Leon, still as stone, close by, both of them staring down into the lifting weed watching for elver.

Reeder's sons we were and both became reeders in our

turn. Learning how to husband the marsh. Learning where to leave the first year's growth and when to cut the second. Cutting, drying, stacking, turning. It was a life complete in itself. And it became all our life. Our parents gone, there were left only the two of us. Used to each other's ways. To the wide sky and the salt wind and the slow world of silence.

Our cottage was set back some way from the track that led up to Pont St Honore, where the ground rose and the marsh gave way to scrub and gorse and low stunted thorn trees blown back on themselves by the wind. The only dwelling in plain sight was Marsat's down where the path ended at the sea. Huddled so close against the dunes, the sea wind could tell no difference and swept right over the top of it without ever loosening a board. A gaunt, grey-faced house, its timbers bleached and furred into soft, curling splinters. Old Marsat was the last of the fishermen on Belle Plage. Every morning he walked up to Pont St Honore with his catch; every morning except Sunday.

We seldom went to Pont St Honore. There was no call, no need; no desire. We had no kin there, no particular friend. We went for candles, twine, matches and cheese. Walking up in silence over the causeway, Leon dawdling, unwilling, behind. Step by step the houses of Pont St Honore rise from a green horizon. Where the track ends, ripples of sand nudge at the start of the gravelled road and little pink stones lie in the grass like fish out of water.

Leon will not go to Pont St Honore alone. He will not go in to Madame Bouride's, not even as far as the counter for bootlaces or a twist of tea, but will hover, head bent, on the whitened doorstep where the brushes hang and the net of carbolic soap and the coils of rope each on their nail. He will not go through the beaded curtain to what was once her parlour. Into the clouded dimness of tobacco smoke and the clatter and fall of dominoes and the sudden dropping away into silence of the grumbling

17

murmur of talk. He cannot be tempted with beer or wine or brandy. I do not press him. The eyes of the men are small, half-closed, drawn in behind lined and folded skin against the smoke. Dark as weasels' eyes in the shadow of a hedge. Their salutation slow – we are and are not of Pont St Honore. Out in the street the women's eyes tighten against the brightness; black pinpoints that glint suddenly, catching the light. They nod with the quick dipping motion of birds. And they smile, gap-toothed, lips drawn back slowly as they greet us, each one of them, watching us behind their smiles. Sing-song voices halt us on our progress down the short street, winding us in first to this one, then to that, the words directed to me, but the eyes never leaving Leon. And Leon, awkward. Sure-footed Leon stumbling in the gravel. From under lowered eyelids, from beneath the speckled shade of the line of pollarded plane trees; sharp, calculating, missing nothing, I see how they watch him.

Old Marsat died. But no-one from Pont St Honore would take the house. Too damp they said, too cold; too far from human habitation. The sand blew up around it burying the front steps one by one. It lay in soft mounds against the door, blunt hands pushing at it, each day in a different position. Grains of sand rolled beneath the crack and blew in thin, whispering lines across the wooden floor, further and further into the darkened house.

Two years it stood empty, holding itself entire against the winds and storms. Only now and then a bit of wood on one of the patched and mended sheds in the lee of the house would crumble, eaten away by the salt, and fall. Till one night towards the end of September, in that season when the moon pulls at the tides and the winds torment themselves into a frenzy; in a night of wind and rain, under the roar of the sea hurling itself at the base of the dunes, and the rattle of wind at the bedroom window, and the squeak and clatter of the branches of thorn trees like so many dry bones being tossed against each other, and the squalls of driving rain at the glass; in and out of dream and fitful sleep, there came another sound. It came in bursts, unevenly. Sometimes singly. Sometimes as a repeated dull thudding. Not sharp and close at hand, nothing to send us out with a lantern, but something far off, something that had its existence there, on the edge of sleep, low and insistent.

In the sullen grey dawn that followed, the marsh lay silent, mirror-imaged. We walked through reed bent low as though before the racing wind, rain-slicked and dark. The light cleared slowly, lifting above the sharpening outline of the dunes. But the marsh was still, caught in a flooded silence like it was held in a bubble. We found our day's place of work, where the Petit Pierre flowed into the Grand Pierre, and set to. The sound of our scythes and the slap of wet reed the only sounds apart from the querulous bickering of geese and the clattering flights of mallard. And then it started again. Loud this time in the silence, sharp and reverberating. Close. Though nothing was close to us, nothing that we could see. The marsh was empty, only Marsat's, grey against its rain-washed dune. From our distance we could see no damage to it, no movement, nothing that hung loose and flapped in the wind. There was no wind, to speak of. The banging continued; wilful, purposeful, with the slap of rage in it. It unsettled the waterfowl. They rose, one after the other, out of the reed and made off south. It unnerved our stroke, till we could do no more. We shouldered our tools and made our way back across the marsh. Now that we moved towards it, it fell silent.

On Marsat's porch the sand lay in scattered heaps, like someone had thrown it. But all was still. We stood at the foot of the steps out on the sandy gravel, Leon tense beside me, taut with listening. The pounding of the sea beyond the dunes echoed up from the sand beneath our feet and the wail of the gulls floated overhead.

'Tis nothing here, Leon,' I said and put one foot upon the lowest step.

We had seen the shadow, both of us, and given it no heed. We had seen it the shadow of something closed. Not something open. With a rush of wind that came from the house itself the door in front of me suddenly slammed itself violently, over and over. With a clanking of scythe and billhook and pole Leon was gone, into the marsh. But I leaped for the door, seizing its handle. I felt it pull against me. In that resistance I felt all the mischief of the night. From out the crack of the door there came a musty smell, a dampness and an airlessness. I could not take my hand from the handle. And I could exert no strength on it. And then – it was gone. Under my hand the door closed itself quietly, the handle turning, the bolt dropping into the lock. But I did not let go again until Leon had found some old twine in one of the sheds and we had wound it tight between the handle and the head of a nail sticking out of the door frame.

All that evening we sat, constrained, listening through the dark for the banging to start up again. Nor could we trust entirely the restored quiet of the marsh next morning, but worked half-heartedly, saying little.

It was Leon who first heard the soft echo of horses' hooves float over the marsh. And then, round the bend in the track from Pont St Honore, above the level of the reed, bumping and lurching in and out of sight, we saw the legs of chairs, the mounding of bundles and the striped ticking end of a mattress. We watched them down to Marsat's. And then we began to walk slowly back across the marsh to waylay the carter as he came back up the track. We stepped out as he drew level.

'See you Thursday,' he called, slowing his horse, 'for the reed.'

I put my hand up to the horse's neck and jerked my chin back in the direction of Marsat's.

'That?' Langlot grinned slyly. 'Why, di'n't you know? That's Jean-Luc come back to Pont St Honore.'

Rain. And the kitchen gone dark as a cave. Sunday rain.
They know all about Sunday rain upstairs. Upstairs,
they act like they're too refined to scream, but inside . . .
Inside, you wouldn't be able to hear yourself think for
the din. Gets to them worst of all, Sunday rain. Taps its
way into the empty hollows in their skulls. They don't
like Sundays anyway. Makes them uneasy and quarrel-
some. On edge. Makes them remember everything that
other days they almost manage to forget. Monday to
Saturday they can keep themselves busy with one thing
or another, there's people coming and going and traffic
outside in the street. But Sunday . . . Nothing moves
round here.

'Such a nice area,' they tell each other.

'Very select.'

'Strictly residential.'

'So . . . quiet . . .'

Quiet as the grave. That's what they wanted. That's
what they've got. And some of them can't think of anything else. They know, on Sunday afternoons like this,
that's all they got coming to them. They see their lives
slithering away like the rain on the window. One rain-
drop sliding after another, one day merging into the
next. Through the rain they can hardly make out the
other side of the street. But they know what it looks like.
Same as this side: white painted steps and white painted
columns and illuminated signs over some of the grander
entrances. The Dene, The Montefiore, Braemar Hotel . . .
All down one side of the street and up the other.

That Sunday the house was silent. Like all Sundays. Hanging. Like a cliff suspended over nothing. Up the wooden service stairs, through the swing door with the porthole, out in the hall, you could hear the dust drop. Pictures of Locarno and the Bay of Naples cut from illustrated papers and framed in passe-partout stare at each other all the way down to the lobby door. But you can't see anything through the twirls of fern leaves and roses on the frosted glass, only the dark space behind the front door. Along the hall there's brown paint over figured paper to the wooden rail at elbow height, then cream. The paint so thick over the bumpy paper it's chipped clean off in some places. Red carpet. Upstairs there's nothing to see either, just locked doors facing each other over landings; no-one there that time of day. They were all in the lounge. Not the first door in the hall, that's the dining room. That's just empty chairs and the thin, sour smell of boiled greens and soggy Yorkshire coming out at you like a wraith suffocating you soon as you open the door. It's the next, beside where the barometer hangs. They were all there, sitting in their accustomed armchairs. In silence.

They'd have heard the rain. Picked up the sound of it at the first drop. But they won't let on, not to the others. Won't let it show. Inside each of them something tightens in the pit of their overfed stomachs, flutters like butterflies in a locked room. But they won't look up; they try not to look up at all – pretend to each other they don't care about the rain, pretend they haven't even heard it. But the longer it goes on, the tighter the silence gets. You can feel it, winding in and out of the heavy chairs and round the brass ashtrays on chrome stands and between the occasional tables. You can feel it wind so tight it goes like glass and if anyone moves, if anyone speaks it'll shatter.

Mrs Blakesby-Judd generally gives in first.

'Oh,' she says, wriggling in her chair, 'raining!'

Any words will do for Mrs Blakesby-Judd. Any sound

brings comfort, most of all the sound of her own voice. But no-one answers her.

The needle darts slower and slower in and out of the folds of tapestry flowers on Mrs Chafer's lap. Endless overblown roses, stool covers and cushions for chairs that she hasn't got. In spite of herself she'll raise her head, drawn by the tap-tap-tap against the window that never lets up. Like the beaks of small, vicious birds. Like long, painted fingernails drumming on the polished arm of a chair.

Over at the table between the two big windows sit the Holy Marys playing pontoon. Every evening after the news on the wireless it's pontoon. Every Sunday afternoon. Ears pricked for other people's conversations and sooner or later the sharp turn of a head and 'Our father' this, or 'Our father' that. 'Our father always said . . .' Miss Biggs on one upright chair and Miss Biggs on the other. Miss Violet and Miss Hett: one strident voice and one insistent whisper. Miss Hett lifts timid eyes to the window, to the writhing streams of water behind her sister's shoulder and licks her lips nervously. She slides her gaze across her sister's face and swiftly back to the card-strewn table. But however furtively she does it, however quickly, Miss Violet has seen her. She leans forward over the cards and her mouth twists down at the corners.

'*Rain*, Hett!' she darts at her.

Hett's tongue flickers over her lips again; she tries to swallow in a throat gone dry. They've seen monsoons, floods, tropical storms – but all with Our father. Orphaned at fifty, now they face the Sunday rain alone. Miss Hett's hands falter over the cards. Her lips bite at each other. And the noise of the rain taps its way into her head, drowning out all her silent recitations of king, queen, knave.

In the sagging green cretonne chair, Miss Willoughby's chair, Miss Willoughby sits staring at the open page of her lending library romance. But her eyes have already lost their place, you can tell. She holds her head too stiffly. The words have all slipped from their shapes and gone swirling and blurring and sliding away, like raindrops. But she won't look up, she won't give in, she keeps her head bent and her neck stiff. The rain has already washed away the story-book images glowing in her head.

Mr Caister in the chair next to her hears the rain, but he sees soil washed away, crazy paving submerged under battered hollyhocks and gladioli piled up like corpses. Sunday afternoon is gardening catalogue time – every afternoon is, come to that. He snaps shut a gardening catalogue, drops it onto a pile at his right-hand side and snatches up another from the dog-eared stack on his left. If he keeps his head down he won't see the street outside, he'll go on seeing his garden. The tea-roses and the standards, the trellised arch, the red-hot pokers, and the Surrey fields and hills falling away under a curtain of rain. Keeps you busy, garden that size. And Mr Caister knows the importance of keeping busy. When newcomers ask about the catalogues Mr Caister laughs, a short, barking laugh, a glad-you-asked-me-that laugh.

'Planning,' says Mr Caister. 'Planning. Can't underestimate it. Not expecting to be here long.' They none of them are. 'I'm just waiting . . .' They're all just waiting, waiting for ships that don't exist to come home. Waiting for dreams. That's all they got now, most of them. 'Just waiting for my investments,' Mr Caister will say, 'then I'll be off. Got it all planned – little place in Surrey, bit of garden.'

He smirks, to make sure you don't think it's just an allotment, or a patch front and back. The smirk says 'acre'. At least.

Mrs Blakesby-Judd smirks too, it's part of the act. They've all got an act on here. Hers is smug, her smirk. It creeps round her mouth and pulls at the corners of her eyes when she talks about the house she and her nephew are going to have one day. Her nephew, Maurice. They've all seen Maurice. He turns up when he's out of cash. They hear about the proposed visit for days beforehand.

'Maurice is taking me out for lunch.'

'Maurice and I are having tea . . .'

But they're none of them fooled, they've no doubt about who picks up the bill.

Maurice turns up in a different car each time.

'Hired,' murmurs Mr Caister to Miss Willoughby.

'How d'you know?'

'Different every time.'

'Well . . . he could . . .'

'Hired!' snaps Mr Caister, the final 'd' spat in her ear. His breath smells like cardboard, like fish glue.

That Sunday though, no-one was saying anything to anyone, no-one was giving anything away. There was just the sound of the rain going plick-plick-plick against the windows like a hail of arrows, needling them. They were watching each other like hawks from behind whatever they pretended to occupy themselves with. Heads going up all at once if anyone moved or there was a noise from the hall. And then going down again, slowly, one by one, wary as scrapping dogs.

They'd been the same all through lunch. All came down in their best, pretending it wasn't. But they weren't just Sunday clothes, we could see. Don't know why they bother dressing up for Sundays. They don't go anywhere, half of them, just sit round looking at each other, same old faces as every day. It's not even a day off for them like it is for everyone else. Their lives are one long holiday, all the time. They get so much leisure they're sick of it. Anyway, there they were, all the artificial silk blouses unwrapped from their tissue paper and mothballs, and the little wool costumes. And Mrs Blakesby-Judd with rings all over her fingers, like the ugly sister off to the Ball. All waiting for their stringy lamb and their roast and mashed and two veg.

We guessed what it was. It was the vacancy.

The week before, Miss Hall had gone down to her

brother's funeral in Leamington Spa and never come back. Just sent for her things and paid off the room with not a line to anyone to say why. That piqued them. Not knowing. Even if it was the disagreeable news of someone else's good fortune. But it didn't stop half of them trying to get her room. Tap-tapping on the door of Mrs Corbett's office, each of them on some different pretext. None of them coming out straight with it. But nothing cuts much ice with Mrs Corbett. She won't give nothing for nothing, specially not a sunny first-floor room like that. By Wednesday the rumour was out that the room had been taken. By a gentleman. A 'young' gentleman. Coming on Sunday, one of them said. So then they all went round saying it. They got so excited you'd think they never saw anyone, nor ever went out in the street. But where they got it from heaven knows because no-one starts here on a Sunday. Mrs Corbett won't leave her sitting room Sundays, not for anyone. You'd have to be dying. Gin and fags and the *News of the World* and ballroom orchestras on the wireless, Bea says, and you could cut the air in there with a knife. Only no-one's allowed in.

So there they were, Sunday lunch, dabbing at their mouths after every mouthful, like they were so refined, getting lipstick in smears all over their serviettes. Patting at their hair. Hardly managing to eat a thing. All except Mr Caister. Chewed his way through the lot, scraping round and round his plate with his knife, sitting stiff as a poker in a celluloid collar and his regimental tie from the Great War. Not much for him to look forward to, some young whipper-snapper taking all the attention.

Made them wait for tea. We're left to ourselves Sundays, only one of us on after lunch is cleared up. Sat in the half-dark next to the range staring out at the rain, thinking of Mum and Charlie and Auntie May. They got so beside themselves upstairs they rang twice. Restless as kittens.

By suppertime they'd worn themselves out, anxiously

fingering the beads round their necks, pulling at the cardigans draped over their shoulders; jerking their heads up at every noise, wondering. They filed into the dining room looking like they'd been cooped up in a railway carriage all day, their clothes all rumpled and their faces sagging. The lowing sound that bellied out into the hall as they came in ones and twos out of the lounge, dropped away again into whispers and mouthed words as they came through the dining-room door. Not in front of the servants. Mouths snapped shut and eyes averted as they pass. Mrs Blakesby-Judd and Miss Violet, Miss Hett and Miss Willoughby, Mrs Chafer and Mr Caister and poor old Major Grandison-Black.

They picked themselves up over supper; over the pushing of dishes backwards and forwards over the cloth and the palaver of condiments.

'Would you pass . .?'

'Can I trouble you . .?'

'Oh, so kind . . .'

Poking with the serving fork at the grey slices of tongue, hoping nobody notices them trying to find a better one underneath. Digging the spoon into the dish of left-over veg gone blood-red from the pickled beetroot. Salade Russe, Cook calls it.

We leave them to themselves, Sunday evenings, though we can't go till they're all settled and got everything they want. But one chair was still vacant and the dining-room door still standing open. Miss Hoity-toit, of course. Who else? Miss Holland. Miss Camille, we called her. One of us saw her name written in the front of a book in her room: Camille Holland, Christmas 1927.

Miss Camille. Acted so nice all the time, so pleasant, so polite. We none of us could work her out, not like the others. They put on their airs and graces and set up their rituals and their pecking orders and you could see right through them. That's what made them transparent – all their fuss. But she didn't do any of that. She didn't give away any clues. Well, one or two, but we never knew what to make of them. You'd go up into their rooms, tidying, and you'd see their things – you can tell a lot from their things. They'd always have smalls out, drying on the towel rail under the washbasin. The others, well you can guess – big enough to wrap two people in and mended and made of winceyette or that brushed serge stuff. But Miss Camille's were always silk and little bits of lace and drip-drip-drip onto a folded towel over newspaper so it wouldn't make a noise. Nothing gets you down when you're feeling low like water dripping off wet clothes onto newspaper. Sounds like the end of the world sometimes, lying in bed in the dark hearing your smalls drip. But not Miss Camille. She didn't belong here, like the others. You couldn't imagine them having any other kind of life. She could have walked right out of this place. The others couldn't. Well, they could, but only into another one down the street or round the corner. One at a shilling less per week, or a back room, or a place lower down the table. They were all of them stuck. They were all of them come up against a blank wall, with only this left to them. But Miss Camille? Some of them said she had money, but if that was so what was she doing here?

The dishes had been all round and the others were sizing up the last scraps of tongue and the red puddle of vinegar and potato and tinned peas at the bottom of the salad. Hesitating. They weren't going to wait all night and they weren't the only ones.

She was still in the lounge, sprawled in her chair reading her book.

'You not eating, Miss?'

She looked up over the top of her book and smiled and uncrossed her legs. And over the noise, that was like a very thin sheet of paper tearing, of one silk stocking sliding against the other, she said: 'I'm just going to find out who dunnit, Edie, I can't possibly stop now.'

'They're all in there, Miss, starting.'

'What is it?'

'Tongue and cold.'

She just wrinkled one eyebrow. You couldn't do it if you practised for a month of Sundays.

'There'll be some left,' she said. Just like that. So sure. She'd never been starving; never even been hungry.

'Well, Miss, there's no more of anything downstairs and the larder's locked. And I'm going off now.'

Course it could have been her ploy to catch the new lodger alone. But if it was, then Miss Camille was going to have to wait all night.

He turned up just before afternoon tea the next day. Bea opened the door to him and came down all of a flutter. When the time came I took up the tea tray. Edging out of the service door sideways with it, all the cups rattling and the Marie biscuits sliding about when the door caught. And there he was, coming down the stairs. That jaunty two-at-a-time kind of jump they do in the films. We met in the hall. 'Young'? He hadn't seen 'young' for some time. Suit just a shade too sharp for a real gentleman, little ginger moustache clipped just too short. Held the lounge door open for me. But not before he'd given me one of them looks – just a flash from down at the bottom of his eyes – gone in a moment, but it was enough. Fancy act for the others and straight down to brass tacks with the servants. Crossed my mind to tread on his toe, or stumble and slop tea on him; instead I got the tray between us so he had to stand back sharpish.

He followed me in. And they all sat up, eager as poodles.

'Good afternoon,' he said. Quite a nice voice. Quiet.

And they all mumbled something.

He didn't put a foot wrong. There were a couple of empty chairs round the room; Miss Camille was missing for one, gone out somewhere, that must have given the others something to crow over, but he didn't make for one of the old biddies, didn't choose between the ladies. Oh, no, too clever for that. Went for the one next to Mr Caister.

'May I?' he said, even quieter.

May I?! Well!

Mr Caister shuffled and growled and his hand went up plucking at his collar as if he wished he'd thought to put on his regimental tie again.

'Caister,' he barked, but it came out like he had a frog in his throat.

'Brookes,' said the new lodger, 'with an "e".'

The others were straining at the leash to introduce themselves, rustling in their chairs with excitement, you could hear them. Watching the setting out of tea like they couldn't wait for it to be over, the cups laid out and the spoons dropped onto saucers and the plates slid underneath. Mrs Blakesby-Judd got beside herself. The door wasn't even closed before she was falling out of her chair, leaning forward.

'Mrs Blakesby-Judd . . .'

You didn't need to see her, you could hear the smile plastered all over her face.

'. . . *Lily* Blakesby-Judd.'

Sladdacoombe, 1971

The sea roars and the high wind screams and the air is white, hazed with the flying salt spray. The shouts of men and the cries of gulls are drowned, snatched away open-mouthed in the roaring. And not half a mile from these wild shores the little dingles are set in the steep sloping of the hills so pretty. So pretty. And so quiet you would not think the one could lie so near the other.

There was a farmer had a wife. There's plenty of tales could start like that. There's plenty of farmers have wives. A wife is a necessary thing to running a farm, though there are them as do without. This farmer and his wife had their farmstead under the shoulder of one of the long hills that ran back from the headland on that part of the coast. But they did not look to the sea. They looked down from their hollow below the lip of the hill inland, to where the grey tower of the church rose out of a net of elm branches and the little dotted roofs crept up close to the wall of the churchyard and the black smudge of the road ran away between them and was lost among the fields.

'Just a step!' Nan Polyard would say brightly. 'Just a step!' And so it was. Going down. No more than ten minutes and old man's beard twining the winter hedges all the way and dog rose and campion in the summer. The steel tips of Nan's laced-up shoes skittering on the loose surface of the steep farm road. Small, heavy steps braced against the gradient, worn black leather shopping bag jolting at the movement. While the fields flowed out and re-composed themselves around her as she descended and the huddled village stretched itself at her approach and the blustery teasing of the wind ceased as the first cottages rose up on either side of her.

It was a pretty village, Sladdacoombe. Travellers are often surprised, coming seaward from the sternness of the moors and the windswept switchback of hills with never a tree, to find cats dozing in sun-warmed corners, the doll-like smallness of the rough stone cottages and the docility with which they follow each other along the village street. It had surprised Nan. Once. Forty years ago. Coming as a young bride to Penbarrow Farm. A town girl. Finchampton. Where the Penbarrow calves went to market. Every market day for a year she and Jeth been walking out, and only his brother Clem knowing and Clem quiet as the grave. One of eight she was, a cobbler's daughter. Never put her hand to the churn. Nor weaned a calf. Nor plucked a goose. Nor set by preserves for the winter or planted out a line of peas. But she learned. She learned so you almost couldn't tell the difference. But the sharp eye could. To the sharp eye she was always a foreigner. Always a townie.

Day after they were wed, Clem announced that he was going for a sailor. A month later he was gone. And that was the last Sladdacoombe saw of him. In a manner of speaking. For at the year's end there was a baby born to Penbarrow. He had Jeth's flattened nose and Nan's dark hair. But it wasn't till after his second year that people began to smile and put their heads on one side and say: Well now, wasn't Davy the spit of Clem?

You couldn't get a word out of him if he wasn't minded to speak. He ran away at the approach of strangers. Into Nan's skirts, or under the kitchen table, or off round the back of the barn. He couldn't be persuaded to venture beyond the farm gate till the morning Jeth walked him down the hill, with his little packet of bread and cheese wrapped in greaseproof paper and tied with string, to his first morning of school. Penbarrow was his kingdom.

He got the reputation of being a thoughtful boy, a good

son. Nan always had on her kitchen windowsill a new posy of primroses or a jam jar of daisies; a jay's feather found in the copse or an ancient whorled stone picked up off the hill. There were other babies born, but they none of them thrived. Bonny babies, but for one reason or another, and some of them thought no reason at all, they none of them saw their first birthday. It was the sorrow of Penbarrow, they said. A sorrow that redressed the balance of riches and brought Nan final acceptance among the women of the village.

But surprise fades into habit. The sharpness blurs, the edges dissolve, like something seen only through mist. Like something not seen at all. Nan scarcely noticed the prettiness of Sladdacoombe now, familiarity had hazed it over. She knew it too well – the curve of its street, the colour of its stones. She could have been a blind woman tapping her way along the pavement; knowing where she was by the alteration of light on her face, the changes of direction in the path. In strange places we are watchful, not necessarily from fear, but from instinct. In his own backyard, safe in his kennel, the eyes of the watchdog close. Sladdacoombe was Nan's backyard.

Tremayne, Rudd, Eddlesham: faint murmur over quiet graves, sibilance of twigs rubbing lightly against each other. Vivid green of the long lush grass waiting for the scythe: mow it down and up it leaps again. Mow it down and up it . . . Eddlesham, Rudd and Tremayne in the cottages going back up the other side of the street.

At Davy's cottage door Nan always stumbles, always loses step. She doesn't try the latch any more. Won't have the street see her locked out. She did in the beginning, when he first moved down from the farm, stopping with a pie in her basket or a piece of cold lamb. She wanted to clean for him, but he wouldn't have it. Took to locking his door. Only one in the village. They'd never locked their door up on the farm. Where had he got such a notion? Sitting in the Ram's Head on the settle to the side of the fire with a pot of beer and a smeared plate of cheese and pickle on the table before him and his sheep-dog at his feet, no doubt. And his own hearth stone cold night after night.

Davy had the running of the farm now, all but in name. Up to Penbarrow at dawn and back at the end of the day to Sladdacoombe again, dusk following him down, creeping at his back over the darkening fields.

Just beyond Davy's cottage was the lane to the Dingle. New Sladdacoombe, some people called it. And new there was, added to the old: new houses, new people. But mostly it was just called the Dingle. It had had an old name, back in the time when it had been a place in its own right. Morse's Well. That was its mark in the Ordnance Survey. That was its name in the memories of Sladdacoombe's oldest inhabitants.

'Who was Morse, Mr Rudd?' Nan, queen of the village, leader of the Mother's Union, president of the WI, organiser of the Old Folk's Thursday afternoons, carried a tray of tea along the row of wooden chairs. 'Who was Morse, then?' said Nan, putting a cup into Dan Rudd's shaking hand. The spoon rattled, a little silvery clink-clink, and the saucer rattled against the cup. And in the withered hand the old bones rattled against the fretted veins, but nobody heard them.

'What Morse?' The watery eyes fixed themselves on Nan, her bright insistent face looming before him out of the clatter and brewed-tea smell of the church hall. 'There never was no Morse.'

'Morse's Well!' chided Nan, the smile glazing.

'Re-morse,' he growled, sucking at his tea.

'What?' Nan bent lower.

'Remorse's Well,' he repeated louder, lifting his head from the cup. 'Bitter water. Brackish.'

'I never tried it,' said Nan, the weight of the tea-cups suddenly heavy as lead, so that her wrists shook and the flesh of her arms trembled.

'No,' murmured the old man, 'nor don't you be a thinking of it.'

But it wasn't a well proper, more a marshy spring that flooded out over a water meadow and twisted away unseen towards the sea. Between the enclosed banks of a narrow stream. Behind the backs of the old cottages and the rotting shacks and the damp-plastered bungalows that strung out along the Dingle path, towards the cove. Towards the light. Towards the wide sky and the sharp, salt-laden wind.

It was dark in the Dingle. Even on a sunny day. A crowding-over of trees and bushes. Thin rasping branches and broken saplings. A dappling on tree trunks, on the path; patterned onto the air itself. Light and shade slipping and sliding so you lost your bearings, lost direction. So you couldn't see your way. See where the path ended and the marsh grass sprang up tufted and green, spear-edged over the invisible brown water; or where the scratch of dead twigs lay and the snare of last year's brambles. The flickering of light and the dimpling of shadow, the ceaseless rippling and eliding. The safe world shifts, moves over. It was the way of the Dingle. It was nothing. Once you were used to it. And you were soon out of it. The trees stopped all in a line and the path stopped too. And you found yourself on the edge of the water meadow, all green soft grass and sunlight and the echo of birdsong.

Like a piece of country, Moira thinks, brought from inland and set down here. You can't hear the sea behind you at all. And the wind that lays flat the stubby grass of the flanking hills and sends the tops of the trees mopping and mowing never touches the meadow. Or the air in it. It's queer, like the meadow didn't belong there. But then no more does she. All dressed up in thin little town shoes and a powder blue macintosh that couldn't keep a shower out never mind rain, and beads round her neck and a handbag in her hand. The wet from the spongy grass seeps into her shoes as she walks across the meadow towards the stream. And the hawthorns by the plank bridge tear at the thin nylon of her macintosh, snag at the limp netting of her string shopping bag. She grips tight to her handbag as she crosses the slippery planks and climbs up through the light wood. Who's going to take it, Moira? Who's going to pinch it? There's no-one else in the wood. There's never anyone else in the wood. The path from the Dingle up to Sladdacoombe runs right through the heart of it; well-trodden, well-beaten, earth packed hard, packed to mud when it rains. And tracks crossing tracks, like a web laid over the ground, running away behind dense rhododendron bushes, threading between beech and young oak. But never another soul whatever time of day you enter it. The old men in the church hall laugh: 'That don't like company, Leeve's Wood. That never has.'

Beyond the held silence that follows the traveller there's always a low intermittent rustling: the slither of a leaf falling, the dry, light snap of a twig. Close? Far off? Difficult to tell. Moira's shoe slips on an exposed root. The path divides. A narrow fork weaves up among thickening bushes over the shoulder of the hill coming out behind Penbarrow Farm. The right-hand one goes to Sladdacoombe. 'Right,' Moira tells herself, pausing for breath. 'Right.'

It's not like Railstone Road, where the corner shop was exactly where she got off the bus night after night. Not like the dairy and the pork butcher's and the little dry cleaning shop just over the street from her office. That's all gone, that's all past. Maisie Thomas and Ruby Forman and Muriel that had the desk next to hers in Customer Queries. And taking dictation day after day from Mr Wix.

'Wixie wants you, Moira.'

'Wixie rang.'

'Wixie says where's the . . .'

'Good afternoon, Customer Queries, can I help you?'

Not any more. There's just the Dingle now. And Louie. Louie gone so frail. And Bill and Vi next door in Sandy

Gates and Mrs T in Shady Nook and Colonel and Mrs Bright in Au Revoir, that Louie said had never been in the army never mind Colonel, and old Lillian in The Shack.

'I didn't know how your cousin was going to manage,' Vi told Moira. 'Before you came.'

Louie, the independent one. Who'd freed herself. Who'd been loved. Engaged. Morning war was declared. Moira could still remember it, and the sick empty feeling in her stomach that in later years she insisted had been at the news of the war. But the fiancé was killed in action. And then both Louie's parents died. There'd always been weak hearts in their family, Louie'd always been thought frail. Her doctor prescribed a tonic of sea air for a few months, see some new faces; get over the shock. And Louie sold up in Bootle. No-one expected her to do that.

'I couldn't have her here!' Moira's mother declared.

But Louie never asked. So Moira's mother never got the pleasure of refusing her and was left repeating her declaration to the mantelpiece. Louie had found the Dingle. She sent her change of address in a card at Christmas.

'Well!' said Moira's mother.

But Moira just gazed into the hissing castles of the gas fire and did not answer. Louie had had everything.

Moira had walked out with Bob Thursby for four years. And then with Ralph Mills. And then, much later, with Mr Figgs. Arnold. That was when she'd joined a choir, thought she might meet some new people. Widower, he was. Widowers always want wives, her mother said. She was rising thirty-nine then and he was almost fifty. Poor lonely Mr Figgs, only wanted a bit of company. Took it, they discovered, wherever it was offered. Her mother retreated into angina, blue round the mouth with rage or pain. Off her food, off the television, off Moira. One day she took it into her head to go and visit the grave of Moira's long-dead father. And had a heart attack climbing back up the hill. Always a weak spot with their family, the heart. They neither gave from it, nor received into it and in the end it dried up on them. They starved it and in the end it spited them. Moira wrote to Louie. And Louie wrote back, inviting her to stay. So began the first of the annual holidays to the Dingle, quickly increasing to include Christmases and Easters.

The house in Railstone Road grew smaller and dingier. The office routine narrower. Moira was forty-five. Then she was fifty. Ruby and Maisie had grandchildren now, babies in photographs. Even Mr Wix had got married. The dairy over the road was turned into a betting shop, the pork butcher's began to sell only frozen meat. Moira trailed home on the bus each evening, the dusty, bumpy, smoky bus, almost empty by the time it got out to Railstone Road. Nothing lonelier than an empty bus on a winter's evening droning on through dark, identical streets. And she set off again each morning knotting a bright scarf at the neck of her nylon jumper, or securing a row of beads. But every morning her heart failed her even as she closed the door behind her. The sound of her key in the lock, turning, the dull click of the bolt shot home. Like a lock being turned on her, shut into her life. Railstone Road had been her whole life. It had not changed. It had always worn its true colours. Only she had not seen them. In the beginning there had been time and hope and all the promises life offered. Promises other people said life offered. Promises kept, for other people. One by one they had faded, dwindled away. Time. And hope. To this . . .

'What d'you do with yourself all day, Lou?' asked Moira that Christmas. 'Down here all the time.'

Lou smiled up out of the folds of the shawl, stretching her old plaid bedroom slippers out over the tiles of the hearth towards the fire.

'Whatever I like,' she said. And she did. Moira knew it was true. 'So long as it don't cost money,' and she laughed, a gurgling, phlegm-racked laugh that subsided into a wheeze.

'I thought,' said Moira, trying to cram another piece of driftwood into the narrow fireplace, 'I thought I might take early retirement. This year or next. Sell Mum's house. But then again . . .' she fingered the imitation pearls round her neck '. . . I might miss the life, the job . . .'

Just before Easter Louie was taken into hospital with pneumonia. Moira came down at once.

'Lou,' she whispered into the grey face. 'I've given up the office. If you like, till you're on your feet again, I could come down. Look after you.'

So there she is, boats burned, down in the Dingle. Happy as a sandboy, that first week. Alone. She spring-cleans the house for Lou's return; scouring out all the cupboards, peering in all the drawers. Lou has nothing much after all. She fingers the damp rising in wavy lines on the back-room walls and above the sink in the kitchen. She knows what she'd do with it if it were hers. Give it a coat of paint for a start, different colours. Get the damp seen to as well. She washes the curtains and the covers on the cushions of the rattan chairs in the front room. The chairs bulge, the gilt all peeled away. She washes the windows and the poky room seems full of sunlight. The Dingle's always at its best in late spring. Leaves curl out of buds, wrinkled and pale green and soft like skin. Along the clinker path between the violets, spears of lily of the valley begin to rise. And out beyond the gate, that hangs lopsided between its rotting posts, there are drifts of bluebells, a hazing of blue all the way to the edge of the meadow.

She finds her way alone up through Leeve's Wood to Sladdacoombe. Not the least bit afraid, so taken with the new greenness and the sunlight.

'How's your sister?' they ask her in the post office. She doesn't like to contradict, not with them being so kind. She fusses with her scarf.

'Improving,' she says.

'And when's she coming home?'

'Monday next.'

'Ahh!' They smile, contented round smiles. It was home that made you well. The crispness of sheets dried in the sun, the coolness of bedrooms under eaves, the soft flickering of leaves outside your window. 'She'll pick up in no time,' they say, 'coming back to summer, like she is. You go up to Penbarrow, get Mrs Polyard to sell you some of her butter and cream. That's what your sister needs.'

It rains the day of Lou's return. Veils of rain that sweep like mist over the hills and run into noisy twisting rivulets down either side of the road. Bill and Vi take Moira to fetch her in the Ford Cortina. It's record requests on the car radio all the way into Trethowan and tutting about the weather and Bill's old jokes and Vi's cracked laughter. And an uneasy silence on the way back, broken by attempts at conversation that all peter out. Lou's skin's the colour of unbaked pastry and her eyes have vanished into deep hollows.

'Stop the car by the sea, Bill,' she whispers as they pass the cove. 'Let's get out.'

'Oh, no love!' they chorus as Bill swings the nose of the Cortina hastily away from the sight of the sea, bumping it off the road, over the Dingle track.

They hurry her up through the dripping trees under Vi's umbrella.

'See you, Vi. Thanks, Bill.'

Into bed.

The house feels different.

'You been cleaning, Moirey.'

The bruise-shadowed caverns of eye sockets turn with the head slowly from wall to wall of the room. The sunken eyes give no light, but they see where the scouring powder has bitten into the scarred paintwork and soapsuds have exposed the watery brown stains on the walls. There are bluebells in a pink vase. Ten. Moira hasn't learned yet about the bounty of nature. Only knows the niggardliness of the town dweller. Picks flowers as if she has to buy them. Louie fills all her wide-mouthed pickle jars with bluebells in the spring, cascades and waterfalls of blue all over the house. And crams all her paste-jars with violets and primroses. And in the summer . . .

'Flowers look nice,' Louie's voice breaks free for a syllable or two from the whispering net of phlegm, the blanket of yellow fog. The words roll like stones, the staccato rattle of gravel pushed and pulled by tides.

Moira stands at the front-room window staring out. Louie's fallen asleep. But her voice whispers on in the air. The house feels different, changed. Louie's again. She stares out, out towards the light, towards the sea. Louie's breathing catches in her chest, stops, with the sound of something caught against a ratchet; like gravel rolling helpless under waves, the little round stones of the cove pulled down the beach, water running away between, washing them clean, washing them smooth. Perhaps that was why Louie had wanted to get out of the car, back there. Feel the sea wind in her drowning lungs, cough up the gravel, spit it out, have the phlegm rinsed away. But they wouldn't let her. The breath frees itself with a staggering gasp.

As Moira stares out of the window the light fades. The darkness comes from behind her, out of the meadow, down from the close-shouldered hills. She keeps her eyes on the point where there is still light, far down at the curve of the Dingle path, out towards the thinning of the trees. She can't see beyond the trees, she can't even see as far as the Colonel's bungalow, but she knows where the end is. Around her the dusk glides, passing over her without touching her, touching everything with shadow. The trunks of the wet trees turn slowly black one by one, their branches etched stark against the remaining light. Lillian's shack clings for a moment to twilight and then is swallowed up. But the dusk glides on soundlessly.

Branch by branch and blade by blade of grass, that's how night comes. And always from behind. In the Dingle.

Different in the morning. The rivulet flashing and gurgling, shimmery as mirror one moment, transparent right through to the brown stones on its bed the next.

'Stream at the bottom of the garden!' murmurs Moira. 'Fancy.'

The wet earth sucks at her shoes the ten strides up to the back door, clinging a little less with each step. Two gardens away, Vi, cigarette in the corner of her mouth, is hanging out undies on the line.

'Morning, Vi!'

Vi shakes her head. 'Don't!' The throaty voice struggling up out of gin-soaked sleep and a breakfast of tea and cigarettes.

Dingle mornings of silence and new light. Breakfast washed up. Shopping to come. Moira's fixed her rituals. Learned that much about life. Learned how to grab at time, snatch it out of the air, pin it down. Parcel it up. Chop it into pieces. Small, manageable pieces. Makes time safe that way, renders it harmless. Gives the day meaning. Purpose. Louie let time slide, go its own way. Louie did what she pleased. And look what's happened to Louie.

Shopping. She strides out. Over the meadow and up through the wood. The rhododendron flowers have all fallen, nothing left on the bush but thick, waxy green leaves, so tall and so wide there could be anything lurking there. Her steps quicken these days so that she sometimes stumbles on the tree roots that writhe across her path.

'How's your sister, then?' they always ask in the shop.

Louie rarely struggles for breath now, just when she coughs. Even the grey has faded from her face leaving it white as paper. But Moira can't tell them. Moira finds other words coming out of her mouth, rock-like words, that someone else – some*thing* else – has put there.

42

'Still got an awful cough,' she hears herself say. 'Terrible, I can't bear to listen to it. Can't get her breath sometimes. You know.' They nod. 'Leaves her very weak.' They shake their heads, looking at each other, looking at Moira, eagerness for more details lurking behind their sympathetic eyes. Nobody's seen Lou since she came home from the hospital. Only the vicar. And the doctor. Doctor won't tell and the vicar doesn't say much.

'Yes.' Sometimes in the shop Moira would warm to her story, the rock-like words slipping out as easy as pebbles skittering down a hill. '. . . very weak. She's still not out of bed. Don't know when it'll be. In fact . . .'

Weak. That's what the doctor says every time, drying his hands with distasteful plucking movements of his fingers on the clean guest towel she puts out for him, like he doesn't want to touch it. He picks up his instruments from the bed, or his prescription pad from the kitchen table, in the same way, as if he doesn't want to brush against anything in the house.

'She's very weak, Miss – um . . . Best in bed a while yet. Get her up slowly, into warm rooms; for meals, that sort of thing, then back to bed. Mustn't go out yet. Chill would be fatal.'

She watches the doctor pick his way down the Dingle between the trees. She watches even when he's long gone and the sound of his car engine reversing down to the main road in front of the beach has faded away into silence over the brow of the hill and Vi has come padding up the path in her tattered bedroom slippers with the stained pink pompoms on the front.

'Well, dear?'

'Chill would be fatal he said.'

'Best keep her inside.'

Moira nods, not smiling.

Vi sips her tea. They sit in the front room with the door closed so Vi can have a cigarette. Whispering.

'You don't look too good yourself, love.'

But Moira's thinking of Lou, thinking of the white face

against the white sheets turning pinker, rosier with the passing of the days. Of Lou in shawls and cardigans and shuffling slippers reclaiming first one room then another. Lou in her old tweed coat with the hem coming down wandering among the trees of the Dingle.

'Best in bed a while yet,' she says in a low voice.

'It's the worry,' whispers Vi vehemently and flicks off her ash into the saucer of her cup with a stained brown forefinger. 'You're pulling yourself down with the worry. You want to get out more.' She leans back in her chair and almost closes her eyes against the cigarette smoke. 'Empties day tomorrow.' She grins. Moira remembers the clinking cardboard box in the boot of the car when they went to pick up Lou. 'We go to Tremorne, make a day of it. Lunch in The Skittles, tea in that nice caff just past Wrack Bay. S'pose you shouldn't leave her for a day, though, should you?'

When the vicar calls, they sit on hard chairs one on either side of Lou's bed. Moira gets out the best cups and puts a plate of Tea-Time Assorted on the counterpane. The vicar has a slow, rich voice; a Sunday voice that makes Moira want to nod off. Makes her shuffle on the stiff chair to keep awake. But Lou becomes animated. A faint beam of the old light comes back into her eyes. She drinks her tea and asks for more and eats several biscuits. The animation lasts for a day or two after the visit and then it dwindles away again. It's after one of the vicar's visits that she first gets up for supper. Moira thinks she can hear sounds from Lou's bedroom like someone moving around, but just as she's about to go and see, the potatoes need mashing and the lamb cutlets catch on fire. Next thing she knows, there's Lou standing in the doorway, steadying herself with one hand on the door jamb. In clothes.

'Well!' she exclaims, and the chop she'd been taking out of the pan slithers off the fish slice and falls to the floor. 'Damn! You'd better sit down.'

It's funny having Lou on the other side of the kitchen

table again. Seeing the familiar head behind the sauce bottle and the blue and white plastic salt and pepper shakers, dipping and lifting, the cheeks working and the mouth opening and closing and writhing one lip against the other as she chews. Quite like old times. Almost.

'I won't offer to do the washing up, Moirey,' Lou says when they're finished.

'I should think not! You get back to bed.'

'No, I'm going to sit up a bit. Put on the heater in the front room.'

Alone in the front room, pumping at the wick in the heater, slowly sliding shut the cover of the matchbox, watching the flame steady and burn up, Moira has the desire to tilt the heater over. Very carefully. Very slowly. Lowering it till it lies on the floor. Till the oil runs out of the reservoir in a quick stream across the lino and seeps into the rug. And the small steady flame ignites it to a river of blue, then yellow, then orange, then red. The flames would run up the legs of the rattan chairs, swing from the flimsy curtains and devour the plaster-board walls with a roar. First this room, then the next – she can see it. Then the whole house, falling in together. She can see it all clearly.

It was the time of day Federico liked to call Tomaso to him to make the day's report. To hear that low, clear voice, that voice like glass, coming to him out of the warm half-light, so quiet, so distinct it might have been the sound of his own thought reverberating in the silence of his head. As if he knew that, Tomaso always kept back in the shadows to speak. He gave his information not with the ingratiating barter of a spy, but in the considered fashion of a man who knows he has knowledge of value. He always brought more than he was asked for, as though the fulfilment of his service was all his life, all his passion. And yet, as the years passed and his preferment increased and with it his power within the Duke's household, an observant man might note also an increasingly sullen droop to his eyelids and an almost petulant fullness to his lips. For Tomaso was bound by debt to the Duke, a debt he could never shake off. Where other men of rank took one of their family as confidential secretary, Federico had taken a stranger, a man who had once been a clerk lent to him from the banking house of an acquaintance, and, in raising him, made him more beholden to him than any cousin.

'And what of the girl?' drawled Federico. The almost lashless lids of his eyes flickered as the reflection of the darting flames from the low hearth gilded him in scale-like lappings of brightness and shadow, where he sprawled in his chair. From the dusky corner of the room Tomaso watched him. He was hot after his ride. Hot in this over-heated room. There had not been fires at Malo, at Malo they did not need them; there was hot blood enough.

'She has – dignity – beyond her years,' replied Tomaso.

The Duke nodded, scarce more than the imperceptible lifting of his head.

'And there were, my Lord, no smiles.'

'Eh? Ah, no smiles, no smiles.' The Duke chuckled, lifting one eyelid to seek out Tomaso in the gloom.

'And she is like her portrait, very like.'

'Yes, de Celsia finds nothing in the leases and contracts, and her portrait, also, appears to be genuine.'

'But I caught no more than a glimpse.' Tomaso looked down at his loosely clasped hands, ran his finger and thumb around the right cuff of his shirt and pulled it a fraction lower over his wrist. It gave him more pleasure not to see, but to hear, only, the sudden shifting and creaking from the Duke's chair.

'You did not . . . ?' Federico never needed to raise his voice, he had learnt in childhood that he only needed to alter its intonation to give it menace.

Tomaso raised his head slowly; he smiled. There would have been few who dared to do that.

'Filippo . . .'

In the firelight the Duke's eyes, turned to him, seemed to shutter themselves instantly with a swift closing of mosaiced gold, the irises no more than a minute, impenetrable dot. A trick of the fire, a play of light on the glassy surface of the eye. But Tomaso knew it was not.

'. . . I sent Filippo. Well rehearsed. I wrote him a pretty speech and had him repeat it to me till he was perfect. He turns out to have an aptitude for such things. I thought I would be engaged for some time with her father, and so it proved to be; now that the time comes for parting the old man is loth to let her go. Besides, if I had presented myself to her, her father would have accompanied me and in front of their fathers young girls are often restrained in such matters, even to allowing their hearts to be moved in secret.'

47

The Duke shrugged his shoulders, pulling his robe closer. 'Filippo . . .'

'Yes,' Tomaso drew the word out until the hiss of it merged with the whisper of ash falling. 'Your page, your cousin's boy.'

Federico raised his eyebrows and pursed his mouth staring down into the fire, shadow and light danced against the slanted forehead, the curving nose and the long, snout-like chin.

'Put some more wood on the fire,' he snapped.

So every day Filippo was sent to Malo with a new present for Donna Emilia in his saddle bag and a new speech murmuring itself phrase by phrase inside his head. Every day the journey seemed to him more desolate: the trees thinner, the light paler, the still water in ditches and channels darker and colder. As cold and dark as the eyes of Donna Emilia. And he would push his horse on with reluctance.

Every day, as he approached them, the strange, dream-like hills rose more sharply from the silent plain, wild and secretive, tangled with trees. And as he turned off the level road to climb to Malo he felt always as if he was riding off the track into new and barbarous country. In such a land, he did not doubt, all the women were like Donna Emilia; all with skin so white, so fine you could see the blood pulsing beneath it like winter streams under thin ice, and eyes black with an almost uncontainable fury. They all, if they spoke . . . But Donna Emilia never spoke. She never smiled. Every day he had to repeat Tomaso's fulsome, courtly phrases to her stone face. And never once . . . They were not his words, it was not his love. And yet . . . Every day as he rode up through the overgrown garden and dismounted in front of the crumbling house he felt his throat go dry and a skein of dread wind and knot itself tighter and tighter at the base of his stomach. As he was shown into Donna Emilia's presence the learned words rose in a babble in his head with other words of his own that he had not even known were there, simpler, more direct words that might melt Donna Emilia's heart. Only – nothing would ever soften the heart of Donna Emilia.

Sometimes her cousin, whom he had seen once or twice as emissary at La Pianta, would be standing behind her chair, his expression as unbending as Donna Emilia's. They played, these children, with the honour of his kinsman, the Duke. And so Filippo became passionate on his own cousin's behalf, ardent in his recital. As the last extravagant compliment died away into the tense, waiting silence of the room, he would kneel and offer her the latest of the Duke's presents. Hold it out in fingers that trembled because they were so close to the stuff of her skirt that they were almost touching it; so close to the long, white, obstinate hands that hid themselves clenched and still in the folds of her dress. And always one of her maids would have to come forward to receive the gift she would not take from his hand. Every day as he stumbled out onto the arcaded balcony and down the cracked marble staircase, on legs that felt as insubstantial as tapers, he saw the opposite flank of the forest rise like a barricade before him and heard the swooping cries of birds among its branches jeer at him.

Every day Filippo returned to La Pianta paler and more silent as if, following their wordless battles, where he felt himself always vanquished, Donna Emilia forced him to wear her colours – her white skin, like a glove on his arm, and her silence. We could observe him from any one of the high windows of La Pianta that looked down over the rear courtyard. Always at the same hour. That hour when the day wanes. That restless hour when the lighting of the lamps is delayed though the script of documents blurs and the entanglement of their endless clauses seems only to obscure further. When we rise stiffly and stretch and lean against the window to watch the last brilliance of the day glow over the flat fields and the black rim of cloud, like the army of night, approach swiftly from the east. Then it was that Filippo would ride into the courtyard.

In the beginning he used to leap off his horse, throwing up his reins to one of the men-at-arms. As the days wore on, however, he took to letting the animal carry him on across the courtyard and under the stable arch, the reins loose over the saddle and Filippo's eyes staring straight ahead of him, as though they saw nothing. When he re-appeared under the arch, he seemed to lurch over the cobblestones as he made his way slowly, almost reluctantly, to the servants' entrance, to where in one of the gloomy corridors he knew Tomaso waited for his report.

In the darkest corner the spider spins its web and there were dark corners in plenty at La Pianta. Tomaso's principal quarters were up in the main part of the house, close to the secretariat, close enough to the Duke's private rooms for their conference at unusual hours to go unremarked by the rest of the household. But he kept also a room, a cubby-hole, down below stairs in that grubby, ill-lit warren where the servants were lodged and where the main business of housekeeping for the great house went on. It was at the end of one of these passageways, set into the thickness of the outer wall, close to a little side-door. A close, shadowed room, dark even in daylight with a narrow window and a lopsided, cobwebbed shutter to it. There were two broken-down chairs and a small wooden chest on which Tomaso's candlestick stood. No bed, no stove. Only the hard chair on which to wait out the long cold hours of night for the soft tap on the window or the light rattle of small stones. For Tomaso took into his hands all the Duke's business.

Into this place of assignation Filippo blundered, stiff with riding, numbed with defeat and cold. When Tomaso, watching for him, saw him outside in the courtyard he would unfold the shutter across the window so that Filippo always entered to darkness. Vast, jerky shadows leapt against the walls and spiders scuttled back and forth in their torn webs at the corners of the shutter.

Filippo stood, swaying slightly, in the middle of the room. Tomaso saw the softness of his lip, the downcast lowering of his eyelashes against the pale, taut skin around his eyes.

'Well?' he snapped.

'She . . . she . . .' Filippo tried to raise his hands, hunch his shoulders, but his hands turned limply outwards from their wrists, the fingers described in the air some vague aspect of hopelessness and fell, lifeless again.

'She thanks his Grace, the Duke, for his gift,' hissed Tomaso thrusting the broken-backed chair aside and striding forward, 'which she will wear next her heart! Isn't that it, boy, isn't that it, for whosoever asks? That and the sweet shyness of her smile, the softness of her cheek . . .' he bobbed his head around in front of Filippo's face and there was a reek of garlic and sour cheese as he came close and darted back again '. . . the perfection of her form.' He drew breath and it sounded to Filippo like the rasp of a knife against a blade. Tomaso half-closed his eyes. 'This – petulance – you see, this – sulky obstinacy – this is nothing. It is so much nothing, that – you have not seen it at all.'

Tomaso moved back behind the candle-flame, his eyes stone-lidded like a basilisk. Filippo thought of the eyes of Donna Emilia welling and glittering, spilling out with fury, and the candle shadows swayed and shuddered against the narrow, grimy walls.

'She is already signed for,' drawled Tomaso, 'sealed and will very soon be delivered. She will then dance to the tune played here. All that went before will be – irrelevant.' He drew his short cloak close around him and from out of its folds his fingers flickered in an awkward parody of the Duke's habit of dismissal, the meaning of which Filippo failed at first to catch. Tomaso scowled at him, jerked his head towards the door and waggled the fingers of his right hand again. Filippo turned, fumbling for the latch and the peevish voice still came at his back, low and clear. 'The trusted servant knows of what to speak and what to remain silent. You are not yet trusted. Take care that you remain – silent.'

Tomaso's voice followed him out into the corridor. Eugenia heard it as she paused in the passageway before the door; they all stopped there, those who were brave enough, to learn what they could. It startled her and she drew back into the shadows. No doubt it whispered on in Filippo's head, each word as round as a pebble; others vouched how he lurched along the narrow passageways, bumping against walls to let them pass, like a man dazed with drink – or fear.

But Tomaso did not move. He sat astride the broken-backed chair staring over the tormented writhing of the candle-flame at the dancing of the shadows on the wall.

*

He had gone away a gangling lad, loose-limbed and loose-lipped with a mouth on him like a whip-cut slashed across his face and eyes that would not hold your own. A late child, a Lammas lamb, they said. And something missing, something wrong in him. His father was promoted from the local gendarmerie to some post at the courthouse in Guy and within the year the elder daughter had made a match with a young man of the town. Then it was we heard that they were trying to send Jean-Luc away. Back to Pont St Honore to board with his aunt's family. But they would have none of him. We heard tales. This and that. In the end the army took him. But even they would not keep him. A line of moustache now straggled above the wet-lipped mouth that still hung half-open. It was not a smile, no more than a dog's lolling mouth is a smile. It hung in its lopsided grin whether he was skinning and disembowelling his kill, or throwing young rabbits live to his ferrets. Or jerking his head in greeting to you on the road. The small dark eyes still watched you close till he caught your gaze and then slid quickly away. But he had a fowling piece of his own now under his arm wherever he went, a fancy foreign thing he was never without. And a dog chained to his door. A thin cringing whelp of a creature never off its rope. We heard its whine on freezing winter nights clear over the marsh and its yelp and the silence that followed.

In winter the marsh lies under the cold, taut as a drum. The smallest sound carries from one side of it to the other, so sharp, so close, as though the frost-bound air had telescoped itself. We kept ourselves to ourselves as we had always done, but wherever we were on the marsh, whatever we did, Jean-Luc was always with us. The more we stopped our ears, the deeper into the reed we went, the more his presence printed itself on the air around us. We heard his hammer nailing runs together out of old boards for his ferrets as they bred and inter-bred. We heard his low, off-key whistling come near and veer away again. We heard the rabbits scream as he netted them at their sandy burrows and the waterfowl rise in shrieking clouds at his gun. We heard him even in the silence. In the way that the silence was changed. There was something in the silence now. The reverber-ation of it was no longer a clear echo, but dulled; muffled as it were, by something in one corner that had not been there before.

Jean-Luc would shoot anything that moved. Just for the pleasure of it. Plover, widgeon, snipe. In October the black geese came, in November the goldeneye. They all fell to his gun. He tired of the waterfowl, varied as they were, and began to move further inland. We heard the echo of his gun over the water meadows and then up in the hedges around Pont St Honore. Larks, pipits, thros-tles, he brought them all down. His face would be flushed with sly pleasure, a vivid, running thing, now rising from his throat to his cheeks, now stirring the darkness of his eyes. Dead birds swinging from a thong hung over one shoulder, or looped from his knapsack. I kept our ways apart. The quickening of satisfaction on Jean-Luc's face glimpsing Leon's pain at the sight of those birds was unmistakable. He drank in the startled riveted gaze, the flinching away and the crumpled dropping of Leon's own head; the hands that jerked unsteadily, clutching at their billhook and pole.

The marsh at night is a place that has its own beauty. For years Leon had wandered there, going out as darkness fell and coming back an hour or so later always with a tale to tell: the look of the moon on the black pools, or the habit of some night creature he had observed. But it was not beauty now that drew him. It was the wire Jean-Luc had stretched between two posts on which he hung his trophies. Leon could not keep himself away from it. Each evening he became more agitated waiting for the dark.

There was no fence round Marsat's place. Naught to stop him. The dog quieted itself at his noiseless step and the babbling of the ferrets scarce rose before it died away again. Through a crack in the kitchen shutters Leon could spy, incomplete, the silhouette of Jean-Luc, his gun broken and cradled on his knee while he rubbed at it over and over, in and out of the crevices and along its gleaming flanks with an oil-stained rag.

One night, as his hands moved from corpse to corpse among the day's victims, Leon found the body of an owl, still warm, its plumage already listless, save where gusts of wind whipped it up into frills and ruffs against his outstretched fingers, soft as silk. His anguish, back in our cottage, burst out of him like dammed water breaking its banks. His breath roared in his throat as he stumbled through the door. His own dog barked at him in fright and slunk away under the table. Leon's fingers fluttered, agitated shadows against the firelight. He turned and twisted in vivid re-creation there before the hearth. Then drooped his own body till it hung limp before me and let fall his head till it lay along his shoulder in that queer, blood-stopping angle of dead things.

Winter passed and spring came slow. Up from the grass

of the water meadows the lapwings lifted themselves, one and then the other, in pairs. A flash of black and white wing-tip soaring and then, hanging on the air, turning, drifting, no longer bird but scraps of silk fluttered on the wind. You saw them lift, wilful and strong, and then, at the highest point of their curving flight you saw them give up that will, saw it go out of them, saw them fall abandoned towards each other, rolling and tumbling, buoyed up and then plunging as the currents of air took them, but always within wing-touch of each other, always within a feather-barb of touching but never quite, folding like a crumpled handkerchief around each other, floating, dropping, then plucked up like lifeless puppets on strings and away, swerving and dancing again beyond sight.

And not the lapwing alone. Jean-Luc began to go up to Pont St Honore on Sunday mornings. We saw him sometimes, a collar to his shirt and a cap on his head. To stand under the plane trees. To lean against a house wall, one foot up against its surface behind him. To hear the satisfying scatter of gravel as he strolled up and down the few metres of Pont St Honore's road. And lift his cap to every girl that caught his eye. He had kin who could not turn their backs to him in the street: his mother's sister and her husband and her husband's brother; there were cousins and young men and women from his childhood. In Madame Bouride's on Sunday mornings there would always be men sitting and the sunlight would swirl the tobacco smoke making the faces round the wooden tables look sleepy-eyed.

There were dances now and then in Pont St Honore, got up for this or that occasion. Jean-Luc tried his luck there too. But for all his boasting of his army days and the cut of his made-to-measure waistcoat, the girls would have none of him. Not even the wall-eyed daughter of Sangsue. They saw how the wine slopped over the rim of his glass as his movements became jerkier. And how a haze of sweat matted the hair that hung down over his forehead giving his eyes a wild look. They saw how the ends of his moustache glistened and how, every so often, his tongue would come out, red and lolling and curl itself up to lick at the wet hairs.

*

He was friendly with everyone inside a week. Put it on just right. Not too much, not too little. And never left anyone out. Never let himself get led into any of their little gangs, or take sides. Clever with words, quick; could turn conversations on the head of a pin. Someone ask him a question he didn't want to answer, he'd deflect them in a moment to something else quite different without their hardly noticing. Just a sort of breathlessness they'd have and a bit of a dazed look in their eyes. Fancy dancing, that's what it made you think of. A sixpenny whirl from one of them pros they had in the posh dance halls, all done up in the proper rig-out with their hair slicked back, twirling these old biddies round, giving them their money's worth, rushing them through the awkward corners in the quickstep against all the other couples coming the other way.

Eyes everywhere he had. Like he had to watch everything that went on in the room. Like he was watching his back – and his sides and his front. Yet you never saw alarm, you never saw the watching. Just these wide, frank eyes, with a smile in them. That was what got them, the eyes. Open, frank look you didn't often still see on a man his age. Wouldn't have cut much ice with my mum. 'What's he after?' she would've said. 'All that smiling?'

Took himself off most days on business. Nobody knew quite where, but it wouldn't have done to ask. Left about ten, quite the gentleman. And some days not at all. That was the classy touch. They loved it, you could tell. Made them feel married, each of them, to him. There he was going off in the morning on this 'business'. And there were they, staying at home. Perked them all up no end. They'd flounce about leaving the dining room after breakfast, like they couldn't think which pressing household duty to attend to first. Sometimes you'd even see one or two of them – Mrs Chafer or Mrs Blakesby-Judd – straightening a picture in the hall that wasn't even out of line. Or moving things an inch or two in the lounge, their hands trailing over objects like they were in a dream, like they were sleepwalking. Like The Marlborough was their own house!

Sometimes he was back in the afternoon for tea and sometimes he wasn't. And three or four evenings a week he'd be out. He generally let drop where he'd been the night before, or the engagement for the evening ahead. You overheard one or two things.

Supper at the Café Royal with a couple of chums. Off to Newmarket.

It gave them the thrill of a life outside their own. A thin little thread to the big, fast, noisy world that probably none of them had ever really known. Gave them time to talk about him behind his back.

It was all you heard first couple of weeks he was here. Wherever you were in the house. Down on your knees in the hall with a brush or going round the lounge with a feather duster. Flick-flick-flick. Gabble-gabble-gabble. Low, like geese. The hushed gabble of tongues and the sharp intake of breath. Mr Brookes told me this. Mr Brookes told me that. And then the voices going loud in spite of themselves at the bits they relished. What they really liked was how he came to end up at The Marlborough with them. He'd been cunning, given each of them a piece of the story so they thought it was their own. Thought he'd confided in them. They told it over and over again to each other without ever getting tired of it. Without ever questioning any part of it.

'Poor Mr Brookes' was all you ever heard. '. . . such a shock. His father dying and everything going to pay the debts of the estate.'

The winter in Monte Carlo for his broken health. The summer in Scotland in a place none of them had heard of, with a cousin several times removed who could offer no help. And now The Marlborough.

It got them all.

Bea would stand at the big stone sink in the kitchen, up to her elbows in greasy water gone grey and cold and shake her head like it was something she couldn't get straight in her mind.

'Poor Gregory,' she would whisper, 'all his expectations . . .'

Bits of old food bobbed around her arms and blobs of fat slid across the water and clung to her skin.

'You mean because he's got to work for his living?'

Even Mr Caister joined in.

'Iniquitous,' he came out with over lunch one day, 'the tricks of Fate. Downright iniquitous.'

They all put down their knives and forks and stared at him. They recognised it straight off. It could've described all their lives, all their situations. They started stuffing it into every conversation along with a shaking of the head and a solemn look. And Mr Caister, every time he heard it, would nod, like he was acknowledging it was his. It was said low, through tightened lips, so that it hissed and bit, all the separate parts of it, snake-like. Iniquitous. They liked it. Like they liked Gregory Brookes's story. It was what they wanted to hear – how life did you down. How, through no fault of your own, Fate dealt – iniquitous – blows. It made him one of them. Course, it couldn't last.

Bea was as stricken as the rest of them.

'Gregory . . .' she would begin, drawling the syllables like she was rolling huge pear drops round in her mouth while her hand moved the drying-up cloth slower and slower over the wet plate. Every day she came out with something new.

'. . . Gregory's in stocks 'n bonds. Dabbles . . .'

You could tell he'd been giving her the eye. Anything's game to that kind of bloke. She'd started dragging her hair into wetted kiss curls with the washing-up water and looking up at you cross-eyed through her lashes.

'Tell you that himself, did he?'

Bea blushed.

'I overhead him, Thursday. Telling Miss Willoughby when I was doing breakfasts. They were both down early.'

'Both down together, eh, before the others.'

Little white patches appeared on Bea's cheeks where before it had been bright red. Her mouth pincered itself into a hard line.

'He and Miss Willoughby's just friendly!'

One evening before dinner, so early most of them weren't yet down, only Miss Camille and Miss Willoughby, Gregory Brookes sauntered into the lounge with the offer of a spare ticket for *Rose Marie* the next evening 'cause his mate had gone down with the 'flu. Turning, as though lost for choice, between the two ladies sitting there he had said: 'Miss Willoughby?'

Miss Willoughby had taken leave of her senses, so the others said. She'd bitten her lip and twisted her fingers in her lap. She'd hummed and hawed and said that tomorrow was Friends' Night at the Victoria and Albert Museum. So, of course, Mr Brookes had turned to Miss Holland, quick no doubt, before Miss Willoughby could change her mind. Of course. Miss Camille. Miss Ice Queen. Who else?

He must've waited days to get those two alone and then . . . Miss Willoughby? Everyone knew she was out alternate Wednesdays. Everyone knew about Friends' Nights; they were just about her only evening outings, all she had to talk about. And he talked to all of them, finding out this and finding out that. Storing it all away. Memory like a card-sharper. He'd got them all worked out. He knew just what Miss Willoughby would do. And there she was, right on cue. Must've been difficult for him not to laugh.

Bea wasn't having any of it though.

'Don't mean nothing,' she said, tossing her head and mincing into the larder with a tray full of blancmanges all wobbling and clinking against each other in their little glass dishes like it was her heart suddenly pounding and shaking and the pit of her stomach gone to jelly.

They said the same upstairs. Only different. He'd got them all so strung up, all so blinded to themselves. Half of them nearly old enough to be his mother, but there they were, sitting in that lounge day in day out. The same old chairs and the same old knick-knacks on their stupid little rickety-legged tables and the same picture vases along the mantelpiece and the clock with the heavy, slow tick. And the rain. And the afternoon dark at half-past-three. Waiting, for their own invitations.

Mrs Blakesby-Judd went off and had a wave put in her hair. Mrs Chafer bought herself a new afternoon gown: plum georgette from Marshall and Snelgrove. And Miss Willoughby took to draping herself artistically in a big Paisley shawl all the colours of mud. Such long fringes it had, they kept getting tangled up in things on her lap and sweeping stuff off tables and dripping into her tea. And sometimes it got itself so wound round her, she looked like she was struggling with a boa constrictor.

They all looked like they were struggling. Struggling with demons. Worms gnawing them inside. But they wouldn't admit defeat. Wouldn't admit they'd been passed over. When Mr Brookes walked into the room and sat down next to any of them they all still made up to him, each in their own way. He went on just as before. And Miss Camille didn't give nothing away.

Nobody said a word. But they watched them like hawks. Never left them alone together. The days passed and Mrs Blakesby-Judd's wave started to droop. And then Mrs Chafer's georgette got Colman's dropped on it one evening. Such a fuss! The stain wouldn't come out and she said it was ruined. It was all ruined. You could see it in their faces. It was all turning sour. Miss H and Mr B were seen coming in through the front door together by more than one person. Or heard. Late at night. Couldn't all have been fluke – meeting on the doorstep out of different taxicabs. The nights their chairs were both empty at dinner and no-one else missing, you could've cut the air with a hatchet. Knives rasped against forks like they were sharpening themselves for a fight, and forks stabbed into plates and disagreements blew up like little paper fires, all flame one minute and crumbling ash the next.

But the game was up when Miss Violet and Miss Hett saw them together one day having lunch in Derry and Toms. The shock of it burst like a thundercloud back at The Marlborough Court.

'Lunching?' echoed Mrs Chafer into the silence.

'Chance meeting,' snapped Mrs Blakesby-Judd. 'Christmas shopping – happens all the time.' She picked up the illustrated ladies' journal she'd let fall on her lap and flicked over a page. 'She said she was going shopping this morning.' Like she'd become Miss Hoity-toit's confidante all of a sudden. 'Said she had one or two more things still on her list to hunt for. She's been invited away for Christmas. To friends.'

That cast them all down. They were none of them going to be asked anywhere for Christmas. They never were.

They came back about four, Miss Camille and Mr Brookes. Bea'd just taken tea up. Such a racket: laughing and brollies being shaken and stamping feet. And then the door to the lounge burst open. Only it wasn't them. It was Mrs Blakesby-Judd, up to high doh. Come for her tea.

'Miss Holland!' she jerked her chin towards the door, 'out there. *Soaking* wet.' She marched across the room and plumped herself down in her chair. 'Caught her death I shouldn't wonder. And her black Courts . . .' Mrs

Blakesby-Judd's mouth curled slowly down at the corners and one by one so did all the others – Miss Violet and Mrs Chafer and Miss Hett. '... are *finished*. I wouldn't have stepped outside the door on a day like today, not if the King of England had invited me. Not in *Courts*!'

Must've been the laughing that got them. Coming in wet through like that and not caring – too busy with other things on their minds. They got nothing on their minds, that's their trouble. Brazen: that's what they thought. Only they wouldn't say it. Wasn't much they could say without giving themselves away. They wouldn't go for *him*, they still wanted him to be their blue-eyed boy. It was her. It was *her* fault. But they couldn't go for her, not properly, not without him knowing. So it had to be the shoes.

Next few days you heard nothing else. We'd never seen them so wound up. At it hammer and tongs, all in loud whispers and speaking without moving their lips so they could pretend no-one knew what they were saying. We came on them all over the house. In pairs on the landing. In twos and threes straggling behind in the dining room when we were clearing up. Out in the hall. Their faces twisted up and their heads together. And the words slipping and hissing – spat almost – between them. We couldn't help but overhear. And when they stood next to the open doors of the dumbwaiter it all boomed down into the kitchen. What they'd wear on their feet and when and what they thought of people who didn't. How they wouldn't never do this and they couldn't dream of doing that. And people – 'people' said loud, like 'you-know-who' – who didn't were no better than they ought to be.

It was all they had. Appearance. Just pretending to a life. Like everyone else of their sort. If you didn't get the details right you'd be caught out. By the others. Because everyone was always watching.

Mr Gregory Brookes knew that. He was careful: only

no-one saw just how careful. Miss Camille had been careful, too. But hers was different. Hers was the kind that
looked like she wasn't even trying, the kind people generally admired. Only now it was slipping. Sometimes you
could just sense it; other times you could see it. Bright-
eyed. Eager, almost, with a new kind of smile on her
face. A sort of leaning forward like she'd found something
she wanted. Like all that Miss Ice Queen stuff and Miss
Hoity-toit had been just covering up the same emptiness
all the others had.

Like she thought she'd found life.

*

She starts going to church. Returning the vicar's visits,
she says it is. She'd been to the church before when she'd
stayed with Lou. Christmas and Easter. She puts on the
hat she'd bought for her mother's funeral, the black band
changed to dark blue. French navy like her new leatherette handbag.

She wades out into the long, soft, early summer grass
of the meadow and feels the jitters start: the trembling
in her legs, and her tongue always wanting to lick her
lips and her heart going pit-pat. Just a silly bit of wood,
she tells herself, as the trees loom. But she knows it
isn't just Leeve's Wood. It's everywhere. Everywhere that
she's alone. She's all right when there are other people
there, people that she can see. It's when there are people
watching that she can't see.

In the churchyard after service she recognises the
couple from the post office and the sisters that run the
shop. She stands with a half-smile ready on her face, but
they're surrounded by their families. Unfamiliar out of
aprons and in their best clothes. Unconstrained out in
the sunshine, squinting their eyes against the light and
laughing. Too busy to notice her, she thinks. She waits.
For Nan. Nan Polyard, stepping through the little groups

with a word for everyone. Head this way and that. Step, step, step.

'Morning Miss Thompson. Your sister not with you yet?' Moira smiles back, her best Sunday morning chapel smile.

'Morning, Mrs Polyard.' She pats at her hat. 'Oh no, Lou won't be out and about for some time . . .'

She watches Nan's dimpled face pulled into a grimace of sympathy. In a flurry of Lily of the Valley, Nan stretches out a plump hand to pat Moira's gloved fingers.

'My dear!' The gold rings embedded in the flesh of Nan's third finger wink in the sunshine. 'You going to walk back with us up to the farm, take your sister home a bit of cream?'

'Well . . .'

'Now, where's Jeth?'

Moira's hand darts up to push at the straggled curls of hair at her neck before she can stop herself. Every Sunday morning like the first. Every time she sees him like meeting him for the first time all over again.

'Morning, Mr Polyard.'

Blue eyes. Bluer than speedwells, bluer than the sky. Bluer even than the sea. They'd never turn grey those eyes or green, or lash to storm. And tall, with a nice way of looking down at you, an unexpected smile that somehow never left his face.

It'd become a Sunday ritual: up to the farm for Lou's cream. Swept up, Nan on one side, Jeth on the other, out of the churchyard, everybody watching. Jeth had such a lazy, teasing way of saying droll things, made her laugh. All the way up to the farm. Made her quite forget the steep road.

'You're late Moirey, where you been?' calls Lou from the front room.

Moira can smell the fumes of the oil stove even from the hall-way. She shuts out the blue day.

'Nowhere. Just up the farm.'

Cream in the kitchen. Coat on the hanger behind her bedroom door. Handbag flung on the bed. Shoes kicked off and stockinged feet cold for a moment on the lino while they shuffle themselves into the cosy fleece lining of their slippers. Hat laid carefully on the top of the chest of drawers. Heart setting up a drumbeat in the silence that follows, knows what's coming next. But her fingers don't tremble on the little gilt ring that pulls out the top left-hand drawer of the chest. They don't hesitate. Down behind the stockings and the hankies, right to the back. They close round the little cold glass bottle, pull it out, wrapped so close with fingers you couldn't see anything was there, slip it into her pocket and close the drawer. Two round wet marks left on the drawer from her fingertips. Sweat drying in the air of the empty room. The coat still swings softly backwards and forwards from the closing of the door. And the sweat dries whorl by whorl of Moira's fingerprints till no trace is left. Not just a Sunday ritual. Getting to be almost a daily one.

Out in the kitchen, Moira puts on her apron. Tying up the strings she edges out into the hall.

'Won't be long, Lou,' she calls towards the door of the sitting room that Louie always keeps ajar, 'you just sit where you are.'

'Smells like it's more than done.'

'Just got to open the can of peas.'

'What else we having?' Lou's voice gone cracked and thin.

'Rhubarb.'

'Not again. That gives me pains.' And then in a low, wheezing grumble, 'Everything gives me pains.'

'It's good for you, Lou. Doctor said.'

' "Doctor said, Doctor said," ' Lou mimics. 'Every time you want to give me something I don't care for you come out with "Doctor said". See you put more sugar in it this time. It was sour as crab apples the other night.'

Out in the hall Moira's fingers close round the tiny blue bottle in her skirt pocket.

'You got cream for it today, Louie,' she wheedles. 'Cream from Nan Polyard.'

And from where she stands, what she can see of the front room looks already empty.

Spring progressed into summer. All night long frogs sang in the cuts and ditches. At dawn, mists lay on the marsh and the sun dissolved them into light that became day by day clearer and more intense.

Jean-Luc did not give up. But he was to be seen more often now in Madame Bouride's than with the groups that stood talking and flirting out in the street. One Sunday morning Madame Bouride came from behind her counter in a rustle of black crepe and, without a word, without expression on her granite face, propped two letters against Jean-Luc's glass. Letters were rare in Pont St Honore. They brought a lull in the general talk. He took them up sheepishly and made to slide them into his pocket.

'Quite a correspondence,' observed Matiot.

Jean-Luc's hand halted halfway to his pocket, his cheeks flushing red for a second. Then he shrugged and grinned.

'Sweetheart,' he said. And drained his glass, scraped his chair back from the table and nodding to those around him, made his way out. His feet caught against table legs and his jacket dislodged chairs he passed.

'Sweetheart!' mimicked Brassien into the silence following his departure. 'Sweetheart! There's not a girl in Pont St Honore will so much as look at him!'

There was a shuffling in the room, an undercurrent of wry mouths twisting into grins, of glasses being raised.

'That was a woman's hand, though,' mused Colbert.

'His mother.'

'His sister!'

'Two hands . . .' went on Colbert.

'Two sweethearts!' burst out Brassien.

Some men laughed out loud and some shook their heads and others sat immobile, dark eyes glinting in graven faces.

'. . . on the same envelope, one on the name and the other on the address.'

The following Sunday Madame Bouride's was twice as full as usual. There was an expectant air in the room. Conversations started up and then petered out again as if the men's concentration was held by something elsewhere. When Jean-Luc entered, a covert watchfulness strung itself quickly round the room. Men did not look at him direct, or if they did, and encountered his own sliding gaze, they pulled their stare quickly from his, transferring it to their glass or some mark on the table in front of them. He did not ask for beer as usual, or even wine. He ordered a cognac. Madame Bouride brought it in a small glass. She brought it and set it down in front of him, where he sat, leaning back in his chair grinning awkwardly. Set it down – and walked away. Out, snap, through the clicking bead curtain. Men's heads turned to look after her, Jean-Luc's too. The glass of brandy sat, solitary, before him. The room became quiet. Beyond, indistinct behind the pattern of yellow beads, the figure of Madame Bouride reappeared at her counter, her head turned, as usual, to stare stiffly out of the door of her shop. In the realisation that nothing more was going to happen, murmur piled itself against murmur. Like water slowly filling a jar. So that Jean-Luc, sitting in silence staring at his brandy as though now he did not want it, was like a drowned man, the waters already risen over his head.

There were, we heard, no more Sunday deliveries of letters. It was not the only day, however, we saw Jean-

Luc make his way up the track to the village. Yet every Sunday morning when he appeared in Madame Bouride's, Brassien would call out 'Hey Jean-Luc – how's the sweetheart?' And the men around him – Lucien, Fardot, Hantise – would spread their legs and lean back in their chairs grinning at Brassien or at each other. But each time Jean-Luc had a different answer for them: one time she was well, another she had been off her work for a day with a chill. And each time there would be in his shambling walk a new tautness that gave to the loose stride almost a swagger, or his sidling gaze would hold your eyes a moment longer. He no longer hung about in the street staring in the direction of some young girl. Inside Madame Bouride's he took to straddling his chair as if he had just discovered mastery of it, laying his elbows along its back and propping his chin on them, a limply rolled dog-end of a cigarette hanging from the corner of his mouth.

'Looks like love,' Hantise would murmur.

Brassien would shift in his chair, turning his heavy shoulders to lean one elbow on the table. 'Love! Him? Fairy stories!' He would jerk his chin in Jean-Luc's direction and lean further over the table as though to impart a confidence. 'He's never been right in the head. And now living alone on that marsh's finally turned his brain. You seen how none of the girls here'll touch him with a barge pole. Phantom! That's all this sweetheart is.'

*

It was the shortness of the summer, they said. It was over by the first week of August. And into autumn. October weather. Nothing but rain, day after day. And a chill that ran along floors and round corners, clung to ankles and settled in your bones.

'Always frail!' yells Miss Pye to Miss Pine, as they stamp up Sladdacoombe's main street together on their morning walk, in identical plastic macs. 'Always had a sickly look.'

'Actually Doctor said,' Lily Thomas winds lavender wool round fine steel needles, 'Doctor said . . .' the words not quite spoken because, really, they should not have been spoken, but mouthed, articulated in an exaggerated way, so that they fall out of her mouth without quite passing her lips and roll among the things on the little tea-table by the fire where Laura Penglowan greedily gobbles them up '. . . first time he visited her, that he didn't think she'd see the spring. So – she did quite well, didn't she? More tea, Laura?'

'I thought she'd pull through.' Vi drains her glass. 'I really thought . . .' she croaks, looking round the circle of bar stools at the lunchtime crowd in The Skittles: Sheila and George, Keith and Evelyn, and Cedric from the pottery stall in the market in out of the rain for an hour lighting up one of his French cigarettes with hands that shake in anticipation of the first drink of the day '. . . for a while that she was almost like her old self. I said to Bill, didn't I, Bill . . . ?' Bill nods, turning from the bar, practised fingers twined round the squat stems of a handful of glasses. '. . . I said, "She's almost there. 'Nother week and she'll have turned the corner." You could see it, kind of spark, trying to break through. "There'll be no holding her," I said. Then next time I saw her the spark was all but gone; all but out. Like you were looking at her through water. And she was drowning. I couldn't believe it.' Vi's voice trails off. 'Thought it was just a setback, didn't we, Bill? Something temporary. Then the rain started.' Around her slow hands reach heavily for their drinks or their cigarettes. 'It was the weather that did for her. The bloody weather. If she could have got away . . .'

'If we could all get away, Vi darling,' says Cedric.

Out on Penbarrow Hill the rain is relentless. Digging with cold steel fingers, drumming and splattering. Pulling at the mud on the footpath. Washing out the grit and the shale, tumbling the fragments into the grass, the slithering, sleeked-back, black-wet grass. Fragments of bone and shard in among the stones, broken bone buttons, bent tin coins. Century after century licked away by the rain. Life upon life. Nobody notices. Davy's boots crash into the grass, over the path and on up the hill. Into the bone and the thick pot chips, crushing them, smashing them, burying them back again into the flank of the hill. The rain darts at him. Lances his eyes with stinging silver needles, pounds at his skull, sings at his ears with pain. And behind him fills up his footprints with water, searching out her treasures again.

In Sladdacoombe churchyard the worms burrow deeper. And the adder glides in silence between the wet stems of the long grass.

At the cobweb-hung door of the cow byre halfway up Penbarrow Hill they wait for the easing of the rain, Davy and Tom. In a harsh rasping of breath still coming quick, and the irritation of wetness dripping. It slides down inside collars, hangs from the ends of noses. They stare out through the grey blur of rain. Like a fog. Like a blindness. Gazing through it unblinking, as if they saw nothing. What is there to see? Only the dark shadow of Leeve's Wood against the brow of the hill. October trees. Forlorn, dripping. The smudged line of the thorn hedge that winds down the hill either side of the farm road. The surly croak of a raven that echoes back up the valley. And then, over the gusting of the rain, they hear a low droning sound that rises and falls. Gets closer. Davy stamps his numb feet against the packed earth floor, digs his hands deeper into his pockets. In a gap in the hedge the snub nose of a grey car appears. Two little black dots in the front seats, one in the back.

'Off out again?' says Tom.

'Huh!'

They watch the grey roof bounce above the hedge lower and lower down the hill.

'She still taking it bad?'

'She still got all her new black clothes on and her hang-dog look plastered all over her face, if that's what you mean. You don't get no alms you don't stick out no begging bowl.'

'Your mum's very good to her, takin' her about. My Dot says she come to the WI now, an' the Busy Bee that knit and stuff for the missions. An' she help out down the Thursday club for the old folks 'longside Mrs Polyard.'

'Oh yeah, she ain't never had such a good time. Thick as thieves.'

'They know her before, then; your mum an' dad?'

Davy shakes his head. 'Total stranger,' he murmurs gazing upwards, narrowing his eyes as if to see between the black drops of rain that fall from the leaden sky. 'Total stranger.'

Everybody talking, everybody whispering. But nobody saying a word. Eyes. Eyes watching. From behind every curtain, from out every head. Watching that softens into smiles when they see her looking. Heads that nod.

'Sorry about your sister.'

And the little house in the Dingle no refuge. No pleasure, like she thought it would be. She feels an intruder there, not its owner. And she had wanted it so much. Had known just exactly what she would do. But the house will not let her. It – holds itself against her. Grieving, as it were, for Louie. She had not thought that walls, that doors, that sullen folds of curtains *could*. There had been no-one there to see Louie's last days. Only them. And who would have thought they could see anything? Who would have thought that inanimate objects could exert such a force – of will?

She begins to have nightmares. Not of Louie. Of the house. Of walls moving in closer. The light, splinter-sound of hairline cracks forming. A murmur of rumbling deep within somewhere, like the rumbling of avalanches. And then the pattering rush of small streams of plaster, falling. She wakes in a fright feeling grains of plaster dust on her face, brushing away at – nothing. Her fingers flailing at her skin, scratching, scrabbling. Subsiding. Into stillness. She thinks she can hear muffled noises. Squeakings and scrapings. Low heavy shiftings. As though something moves with difficulty along the floor in one of the other rooms. Something . . . unused to movement. In other parts of the night she lies wide-eyed for what feels like hours. Watching the darkness change shape in front of her; blackness detaching itself from blackness, advancing and then receding.

In the mornings she wakes heavy-eyed to the same grey dullness. To the drip of rain and a watery half-light filtering through the spindly trees of the Dingle. To the distortion of her face in the spout of the kitchen tap as she fills the kettle for her tea: the mouth pulled wide, greedy and thin-lipped; the eyes small, no more than dots; the nose twisted out of line. The accusation of the single cup and plate and knife. And the sounds of the tea caddy being prised open, the bread being cut, the lid of the marmalade jar being twisted off fading away into silence. A silence that follows her from room to room. A silence she hears however loud she turns up the volume on Lou's old wireless. She goes out into the garden, and the silence seems to have got out there before her. Only there it is another silence, the silence of the Dingle.

In the November fogs the Dingle is held in stillness. So white, so muffled. It presses against the window pane. It clings to you the minute you step outside the door. Wrapping itself around you, making you cough. Making you gasp for breath. And then it's inside you, acrid and sour. The Dingle becomes a ghost world. Where the trees fade even as you look at them. And the houses beyond old Lilian's are gone, disappeared into nothingness. Moira doesn't try to find them any more. She knocks once or twice on Bill and Vi's door, but nobody answers. Last time she called there the Colonel put his head over the next-door fence, gave her a funny look. Watched her all the way down their path. Seeing her off the property. The cheek of it!

*

Mr Brookes went off the day before Christmas Eve. To friends, he said. You could've heard a pin drop when he broke it to them. The dining room went quiet. Hollow. Like something had pressed down on them and squashed them all to the floor, something they'd been expecting so they none of them struggled, they just gave in. Her going off. And now him. And both to 'friends'. Their last chance to get things back to where they wanted them, gone. No-one asked where or for how long, or any of that how's your father, though you could see he was expecting it.

Christmas lunch, we moved the two empty chairs out of the dining room and spaced the settings out to cover up. But it didn't help much. They all sat about in their best with nowhere to go, like Sundays only worse. Mrs Corbett came down for lunch and we gave them goose and all the rest of the palaver. They wore their tissue paper hats and read out their mottoes. That cheered them up a bit. But they were back at their squabbling by teatime.

Boxing Day it rained.

And then there was just January stretching away in front of them, flat and grey and cold. Supposed to be a new year, but it didn't look much different from the others.

Miss Hett saw in Mr Caister's paper that they were demolishing the Empire. She read it out. All excited. Like it was all the theatres in London being knocked down.

' "End of an era . . ." it says.'

End of all their little outings, they thought. And their eyes lit up. And then dimmed again. There wasn't going to be no end. If it wasn't theatres, it'd be dancing or cinemas or suppers up West.

They came back from Christmas, Miss Camille and Mr Brookes, with a regular old pals act. Discreet you could've called it. But you could see he couldn't wait to get his foot further in the door. And she looked like she was already out of her depth. Pleased with everything she was and laughing, like it was all a joke. Got in front of herself. He'd worked hard to get her that far, but it didn't stop him playing his little games with Bea in the dark corners of the landing or the turn up to the top stairs. A pinch and a wink; something murmured as they passed that made the colour shoot up into her cheeks. You got to hear the laugh, low in his throat, that he did, even below stairs, like some sixth sense warning you. Minute later Bea'd come clattering down, cheeks red, eyes not looking at you.

'You'd better watch yourself,' I told her.

Somebody should've said the same to Miss Hoity-toit. Only she'd already got beyond it.

It wasn't till he took Miss Camille to a dinner dance that they really took against him. She came down to the lounge in a cloud of aquamarine chiffon and spangles. All breathless. He leaped up when he saw her.

'Well!' he said, smiling at her one of his matinée idol smiles. And then, turning to the others, he grinned at them, all boyish. 'Isn't she a picture?'

But they'd seen. One smile for her. And another for them. That did it. They squeezed their mouths, unwilling, into lemon-rind smiles.

But the spangles still glittered in the room long after Miss Camille and Mr Brookes'd gone. They danced against their lowered eyelids like fireflies buzzing, the blue cold as the night, and the smell of frost and wet that rushed from outside into the lounge making them shiver. And her scent fading slowly along with the bang of the front door.

It was a couple of hours later that Mrs Blakesby-Judd lifted her head from laying out her patience cards. But as none of them had said a word in all that time, it was like the continuation of a conversation that they'd all been having silently.

'I wonder,' she said, and their heads all went up at the sound of her voice, slow it was, deliberate and thin-edged like the blade of a knife seeking its target. 'I've *always* wondered how he has time to do any business with all this gallivanting about – whatever his "business" is. I've never heard him say, precisely. Have you, Mr Caister?' Her chins were wobbling up and down with the excitement and she was shuffling in her chair like she was urging the others on to follow her.

'Not – precisely.' Mr Caister's fingers fumbled at his tie-pin.

'Something in the stock market,' piped up Miss Willoughby.

Mrs Blakesby-Judd looked daggers at her.

'Something! What?'

Miss Willoughby shrugged her shoulders and a small nervous smile fluttered for a moment and then vanished from her thin lips.

'Something ... or other ...'

Then Mrs Chafer had a letter from a friend in Rutland who'd never heard of Mr Brookes. Or his father. Or any business over an estate called Madinglea.

'Of course,' said Mrs Chafer quickly, 'it doesn't mean a thing. Rutland is our smallest county, but I'm sure you still couldn't know everyone.'

But it got whispered round among them. Changed day by day. Into a certainty. That no-one in Rutland had heard of him. Whisper, whisper and then the quick shutting up of mouths. Better than a game of Grandmother's Footsteps it was. And little Grandmother Camille all unsuspecting. They weren't going to tell her. Sitting there in her dove-grey chenille blouse, or her brushed merino twinset with her Mudie's library book on her lap and her silk-stockinged legs crossed just so at the ankles.

They started going round, all of them, like they were

rolling acid drops on their tongues. Their cheeks sucked in and their mouths pursed one minute and innocently flat the next. Mrs Blakesby-Judd was the boldest, her eyes gone small and bright and mean.

'Is that so?' she began saying whenever Mr Brookes told her of some new jaunt. 'Is that so?' Raising her eyebrows and turning the ends of her mouth down just slightly and her eyes not lifting, usually, from what she was doing. First time she did it, the silence in the room went tight as a drum, all the others paralysed with excitement in their chairs. But he didn't lose a beat.

'Yes,' he said. Like it was interest she'd shown.

But clearing Miss Hett's plate, opposite him, you could see, you could catch just a glimpse of blankness and then a scurrying like shadows in his eyes. And then, quick as a flash, it was all covered over.

'All this Buffy and Algy and Percy. And this here and there,' said Miss Violet, standing in front of the fire a couple of mornings later. 'But he never gets any post, so how does he receive all these invitations? Never has any telephone calls.'

'And all this talk of Lagondas,' added Mrs Chafer, 'and runabouts and goodness knows what! But we never see a car stop at the door.'

They took to it quickly. Bit of spite to warm a cold winter's morning. They had nothing to go on, nothing much. Just little things. Things that if you were watching for them made you think – hullo, what's that? And they were watching. From then on.

He must've known something was up. Something different. She didn't see a thing. He was whirling her round so fast she might as well have been blindfold. But she was cleverer than we gave her credit for. If they weren't giving anything away, then neither was she. And none of us would've known a thing if Bea hadn't come prancing into the kitchen one day and said she was giving notice.

'I'm going up north,' she said.

'Up north! What for?'

'*She* asked me.'

'Who?'

'Her. She's going off. With him. She's got a place, a house. Up in the Lakes she says it is. And they're going there and she wants me to be her lady's maid. Well — maid, but there's going to be local help and that for the kitchen.'

'You must be barmy. When're you going?'

'Tomorrow week. Only I'm not to speak of it. And you mustn't tell a soul, or I'll lose my place.'

'What's she ask you for?'

Bea tossed her head.

'P'raps,' she said, with her chin in the air, 'p'raps she thinks I'll do a good job.'

'Yes, and p'raps *he* thinks you'll do a good job an' all. You watch yourself, Bea, up there alone. They're not married and, you mark my words, you won't see them married either, whatever they tell you.'

But, of course, she didn't want to listen.

*

The day of the betrothal ceremony came and Filippo, setting out for the familiar journey to Malo, now found himself surrounded by a jostling, glittering party of horsemen, carried along among banter and laughter and eager expectancy in a silence that was no longer bemusement, but knowledge. He knew the stand of spindly, yellowing trees at which the road branched; he knew the echoing span of the bridge over the canal marking the halfway point, that threw the quick, syncopated clatter of their passage out over the flat, dark fields and drew it back in again to reverberate under the stone arch. At the first sight of the strange hills the men around him pointed them out to each other with exclamations of amused curiosity, but he felt only the tightening of dread. He knew it could not be far now to the beginning of her father's land. And he knew that when she came to meet him, when she left her hills and her people; when she stepped beyond the boundary of her father's land . . . then she was lost.

The way narrowed and then widened. In the stringing out and the re-grouping he found himself jostled closer to the head of the party. He could now see Tomaso in front of him, the stiff velvet pleating of his cloak collar turned up against the chill. He could see the Duke and around him the heads of his close kinsmen. Heads that turned this way and that like paper cut-outs turning, all the same head, slant-browed, long-nosed, laughing, calling to one another; the same eyes glancing around at the country through which they passed. Those eyes that in the last days had begun to regard him with a new watchfulness. Filippo tried to drop back out of the Duke's sight, but the press of riders behind him was too eager and he was carried on like a cork before a wave.

It was a day heavy and still, cold with the sense of fogs rolled in across the lagoon from the sea, a held, muffled feeling to the air. Around the gaiety and swift trotting of the Duke's household, the wet fields stretched away into an endless greyness, the whole party no more than a tiny moving blob of colour on the wide, flat plain. And then, suddenly, moving towards them, there could be distinguished another dot of colour, one that flowed out from its boundaries and was drawn back again and, dancing before the eyes, became gradually larger and more distinct. Afterwards, no-one could agree whether they had first heard Donna Emilia and her ladies, or seen them. For out of the cold air there came a high, sweet sound like the sound of glass singing. There was a dropping away of banter and laughter, the uncertain slowing and bunching up of reined-in horses. Still the sound came on, a tinkling of hundreds of tiny silver bells tied to the ladies' saddle-cloths and the plaited manes of their horses, which grew louder and louder. Then there they were, facing each other across a ploughed field. Like two small armies. Like opposing teams at a jousting; gentlemen and ladies gathered in this wintry place for some Christmas game. Both sides rode slowly forward, as was the custom, till there was no more than half a field's width between them and there they paused. There they waited for Donna Emilia to ride out to greet her betrothed. To place her hand in his, plighting her troth, and lead him across the boundary of the two fields onto her father's land where he would become master, as he would become master over her.

In the silence that fell and lengthened horses breathed noisy clouds of warm breath into the air and jangled their bridle-chains, small impatient ripples of sound. All eyes were on the grey palfrey and its scarlet-cloaked rider who still sat immobile. There was the faintest prickling of unease, as swift and sinuous as the passage of a snake through the company. A whispering of ill omen that silenced itself as soon as it was thought, becoming no more than a breath, a rustle, passing over people's heads. Hands that were raised instinctively to cross themselves were quickly snatched back into sleeves of doublets, or hidden inside cloaks. No-one dared to glance at Federico, who stared, unmoving, before him. Only Tomaso, under the guise of looking down at his right stirrup as though to check its position and then surreptitiously raising his eyes in the way that he had, watched his master from under lowered lids. Filippo stared at the ground, at the soft, crumbling ridges of the ploughed earth.

All at once, stumbling a little, trotting forward, halting sharply, then going on again, Donna Emilia's palfrey moved out onto the field. The women clustered either side of her separated suddenly, their horses dancing sideways as, from the rank behind them, two of Donna Emilia's kinsmen broke forth. They rode close to the flanks of the palfrey, looking neither at each other or their young cousin, but straight ahead, riding so close against the palfrey's rump it was almost as if they carried it forward between them. On they went, on into the centre of the field and there they halted. Curling one gloved hand into the fur lining of his cloak and with the other loosing his tightly pulled back reins, Federico permitted his black horse to move into a slow, magisterial walk. Suddenly, with a papery clatter of wings, a flock of fieldfares flew up, so quick they seemed more like a blown scattering of leaves that somehow held themselves in formation. They flew up against the light, dark, for a moment, as a cloud; then dipped, invisible with the light now on them and, banking into vision once more, became birds again with small brown wings. Donna Emilia's eyes had caught their first swift ascent. She craned her neck to watch them bank and turn and the hood of her cloak slipped down and her hair fell loose round her shoulders. She twisted in her saddle to see them fly against the light and then, as not their shadow but the Duke's fell across her, turned sharply back.

He withdrew his hand from within his cloak and as he held it up a cascade of pearls fell from it in a long rope. Laying his reins over his saddle, he leaned towards her. It happened all in a moment. Like a net flung. The pearls high in the air against the pale oyster-shell sky as if returned for a split second to their element. She did not flinch as they dropped around her neck, though their touch must have been cold as sea-water. She did not move. She could not. Hemmed in by her kinsmen at the back and by the Duke at her front. First the pearls and then the ancient, heavily worked gold chain set with garnets. The wealth of the House of Piacenza e Lusia from sea and land bestowed on her.

It was not clear whether the girl put out her hand to the Duke to lead him onto her father's land and back to her father's house, or whether he had to take her hand in his. But the cheer that went up from the assembled company was ragged, half-hearted and only gained strength on the final huzzah. Few were taken in by the business with the palfrey. And all had seen how her heart flew with the fieldfares. There were those who said the marriage should not take place and others who, knowing the pride of Duke Federico, said it would not. Only her father, astride a great bay, beamed and nodded as though he saw nothing.

It was cold, Bea said. Cold and rainy. And the hills crowded in wherever you looked, black, and the sky black above them all except for a thin line along their tops, white like silver. And a queer polished light reflected up out of the lake beyond the town. And Miss Camille not Miss Camille any more. But Mrs Brookes. A new gold ring on her finger. And a new tweed coat with a huge fox fur collar wrapping her like a cloak. And all the tradesmen rushing to hold the doors open for her in every poky little shop along the High Street. Out of one and into another. Miss Camille sweeping along all smiles and scent. A dozen of this and a dozen of that. Bea scurrying behind her. And shop girls watching from the gloom behind counters, wide-eyed some of them and others giggling behind their hands, nudged into 'Good morning, ma'am' in peculiar sing-song voices that made everything a question.

They didn't go to Fernlea straight off. There'd had to be workmen sent out. The roof leaking over one of the bedrooms and some of the windows letting in rain. Nothing much, just what you'd expect in a house that hadn't been lived in for so long. Funny Miss Camille having it all this time and never mentioning it. Funny having a house and not living in it.

They had to stay in The Blue Boar when they first arrived. Bea didn't like it much there. She had to fetch up Miss Camille's breakfast tray from the kitchen and eat with the staff. They leaned round the long table towards her, watching her with sharp eyes. And questioned her in voices that danced away from her so that she could hardly follow them. But she saw, by the expressions on their faces and the way that one speaker turned to another, that these were not questions at all. They seemed to know all about Mr Brookes without ever having clapped eyes on him. They knew whose cheque was in his pocket and why he stayed in London and even that he was younger than Miss Camille – though what business of theirs it was, so slight a thing, Bea said, she couldn't think. They knew when he'd be joining them in Keswick, too. Though it wasn't at all the same as Miss Camille had told her. But when Bea contradicted them they went silent and looked at her like she was an uppity child who was best left to find out the truth for herself. And when she said nothing they smiled their slow, thin-lipped smiles at one another, taking her silence as proof of assent.

Mr Brookes had stayed in town to take delivery of the new car Miss Camille had ordered. We couldn't possibly manage up here without a car, she said. But Bea knew that it was really for him; his idea too, no doubt, put in Miss Camille's mind. And Miss Camille's money paying for it. But first off there seemed to be a mix-up over the delivery dates. Mr Brookes insisting they had said one date and the showroom saying they had another in their order book. So there they were, stuck up in Keswick, the days going by and Mr Brookes ringing from London every other evening with something else delaying him.

They swept in and out of shops till there was nothing left for them to buy. And walked what seemed to Bea like miles along the lake in the afternoons. Bea could hardly catch what Miss Camille said to her on these walks, the shiver of cold in her head seemed to drown everything out, the wind snatching up the words and the little glinting waves of the lake scattering them in a glitter far out over the water. But before long Miss Camille's cries of 'Isn't this place heaven?' 'Isn't it beautiful!' lost their shriek of enthusiasm. And her face took on a shrouded, anxious look when she thought no-one was watching. There they were, after all, stuck up in goodness knows where and freezing to death and all for him, all so they could be together.

Every day, Bea said, she expected to see him drive through the narrow streets of the little town everything scattering before him. Every time she heard the hammering roar of a car's engine she'd look up eagerly, sure it was him. But it never was. Miss Camille didn't seem to like the Blue Boar quite as much as she had before. Perhaps she saw something behind the attentive gaze of the dining-room staff. Perhaps she caught their knowing smiles. Or heard words sliced off and swept backwards on a puff of air from one of the swing doors to the back stairs or the pantry.

When the builder came to report progress on Fernlea and said there was only the scullery roof left to do, Miss Camille said never mind the scullery, the scullery could wait, but that she had waited long enough and intended to move there at noon the next day. She had notes sent off within the hour to the carter and all the various provision merchants. And the bell-boy sent round to the maid of all work and the cook she had hired to tell them to be ready at the carter's first thing in the morning. She put through a call to Mr Brookes's hotel – he hadn't stayed on at The Marlborough – but of course he was out. You could tell what had happened the minute she came back upstairs.

'Well!' she said, slamming the door of her sitting room, 'He'll just have to find us!'

They went by pony trap, it was such a nice day. Blue for the first time, sharp and clear. Like a good omen. Driving out on the little brown road with the hiss of dead leaves fluttering away on either side of the trap wheels and bowling along in front of them, Bea felt almost as excited as Miss Camille. The cook and the scullery maid and the luggage all gone ahead in a motor van at the crack of dawn.

'Not far,' said Miss Camille.

But at every turn of the narrow road first the town was lost, then one by one the big houses behind their beech hedges and thick wet clumps of rhododendron, and then even the white dots of cottages on the opposite hills. They bumped off the road onto what was no more than a gravel track. It ran near the lake for a time. Just the lap-lap of water, black and silver in the shallows and the cold hanging cry of a bird that echoed like they were all caught in some closed space. And the creaking of the big iron wheels as they bit into pockets of sharp stone and bounced over the frost-hardened ruts of mud.

They turned inland and the hedges ran close; the low whispering of dead leaves loud now in their ears and the spines of the hedge thorns scratching the trap. And then they were through rusted gate posts and a white gate propped wide, and the drive opened out, flat and smooth.

The house was silent when they entered; the motor van unloaded and gone away, the front door open and sunlight lying quiet over the hall floor stained blue and red from the coloured glass. A smell of damp came out at you. A smell like wet paper. Like something you could reach out and touch. Miss Camille wandered from room to room, opening door after door, without stopping, as though she was sleepwalking. Smiling. Bea trailing after. One flat, faded room after another, all with that close musty smell like old breath. All with a wisp of smoke wavering and falling in their cold hearths. And dead flies fallen beneath windowsills to the floor. There were books lying about, their covers bleached from red to pink and magazines gone scorched. Shoes on their sides under a chair up in a bedroom like they'd just been kicked there. And slivers of soap still in their soap dishes on washstands, their waxy backs arched and cracked and little bubbles where the last person had washed their hands dried onto their surface, lying caught there still, under the dust.

White paint had faded to cream. And cream to yellow. In some corners there was mould over the wallpaper and tears at the edges where it joined. There was mildew up the legs of the cane whatnots in the living room, the magazine racks and the wobbly tiers of occasional tables. And wherever you went in the house, sticky skeins of spider's web that brushed at your face and caught, for a moment, at your leg before you felt them tear and float suddenly free.

Bea didn't like it there at first. She didn't like the silence. And no-one calling, only the butcher's boy once a week and the grocer's van and a child from the nearest farm every day with milk. And no sight of a house except shepherds' cottages the size of pin-heads on the far hills.

'What about the big houses we passed on the road?' she asked Mrs Pikes and May in the kitchen.

'Oh, they won't come up till Easter, p'raps not till the summer,' they said.

And there was a wind that soughed, starting up in the silence. A low lifting and falling of thin noise that dropped to a sigh, broke off for a second and started up again, louder. A wail sometimes. Almost a cry. Sometimes just murmuring, moving from room to room; winding around the legs of chairs and tables, lifting rugs in passageways with a low flutter. Hunting. Miss Camille would set off round the house, looking for the cause of it, the hole, the crack by which it came in. But she never found it.

Always something invisible touching you, Bea said. And the chill never quite taken off any of the rooms. But *she* liked it.

'Spent her childhood here, in the summers,' said Mrs Pikes. 'She and her brothers.'

You could see it, Bea said, in her eyes. They were full of it. So that wherever she looked she didn't see it plain, but overlaid, wrapped snug and cosy at the edges with memory. Everything safe; everything with another meaning, a little story to it – where she'd done this and where she'd done that. She didn't feel the stinging chill in the rain that blotted out first the lake and then the stands of trees at the edge of the garden.

'Beautiful, Bea, isn't it?' she would murmur standing at the big picture window. 'Beautiful.'

And Bea would turn obediently and stare, too, out of the dull, faded room where the dark already hung, over the bleached grass of the lawn and the bare trees to where the light flared and then died along the folded hills.

She was in seventh heaven. Till the telegram came. Bea had to take it to her, with the boy still waiting at the open door. She flung it down in a rage.

'Is there any reply ma'am – while the boy's here?'

But Miss Camille turned on her such a face, Bea's words died in her throat. She'd never seen her sharp before. She marched over to the bureau and pulled out a sheet of paper so hard all the other notepaper fell out with it. She snatched up a pen from among the writing things on the little tortoiseshell tray.

'No. Tell him to take this note to the bank.'

But she'd written no more than two words when she threw the pen down again.

'Send him to Prothero's! I want the trap out here first thing tomorrow!'

Bea didn't dare look up to see her face. She couldn't raise her eyes from the sheet of paper that in Miss Camille's hands was being crushed and squeezed and rolled into a ball.

'What'd it say, Bea?' they asked her in the kitchen. 'The cable?'

'I couldn't see,' said Bea, though she'd caught a glimpse. 'It was folded up.'

'That's money,' Mrs Pikes shook pounded sugar over the cloud of beaten egg white in the bowl before her till it was a glinting, sparkling mass, 'sending notes to the bank. And then not a letter – letter won't do – but she must go herself. He's sent for money. That's what it says.'

'She didn't say,' said Bea, drawing up her own mouth tight. But Mrs Pikes scarcely paused.

'She sends him money she won't get him up here in a hurry.' She picked up a spoon and drew the cloud round and round upon itself until the sparkling was gone and it became thick and viscous. 'She wants to start as she means to go on. Don't he have no money of his own?'

But he was with them by the Wednesday. Bea felt it like a triumph. They heard the roar of a car engine out on the drive and the gravel spring up and clatter down again at the front door. In the kitchen they stood stock still, looking from one to the other, eyes all enquiring and smiles sliding, with the realisation, along their mouths. They heard the burst of his voice in the hall and through the rooms, booming and rising like shouting. Like before there'd been only silence. Like none of them had spoken for days, all life gone out of them, flimsy as ghosts till he should appear.

It wasn't reading novels in front of the fire any more. Or mooning about the wet garden, her coat hugged to her, stopping at the jasmine broken out into stars on the sheltered wall, or the snub-nosed clusters of bulbs come up in the long border and down the drive. Or watching the birds run about on the lawn. He didn't care for all that. And so, all of a sudden, neither did she. She never gave a thought more to it, you could see. She didn't have the time for it, Bea said, and no more did they. If it wasn't breakfast he wanted it was elevenses and then lunch and then what was there for tea? Always there had to be some treat. And when one was over he had to be on to the next.

Wet days he'd have her playing all sorts of games. Over and over. Silly games Bea wouldn't have thought she'd bother with. Board games he'd found in the cupboard and guessing games and the like. Fine weather, they were out in the car, here and there wherever there was a road fit to travel. He had her dress for dinner, though there was never more than the two of them. And made Bea hunt out all the candlesticks she could find and put them about the dining room. Miss Camille looked nice by candlelight, her eyes softer and darker. She laughed at him, from her end of the table, but you could tell she liked it. And never a word, as far as Bea heard, about what he'd been up to all that time in London. No reproach.

One day they came back from a jaunt to Kendal with silver shakers and funny-shaped bottles of goodness knows what: blue one of them and another green and two with no colour at all. And jars of cherries in what smelled like perfume and tins of different salted nuts. From then on every night it was cocktails. At six o'clock sharp Bea had to lay out scallop-edged paper coasters and coloured cigarettes with gold paper bands and dishes of salted nuts. And down he'd come – always down before *her* – rubbing his hands and looking eager.

'Well, Bea, where's the ice?' he'd say. Or 'Bring me another lemon.' That's when he started up the chat again. She didn't take much notice at first. Just blushed and giggled and got herself out of the room. She was always in a fluster those first weeks, so much new to learn.

He'd mix up this and that, a new concoction every night, and fit one of the coloured cigarettes into the silver holder Miss Camille'd given him. Then she'd arrive. She hardly touched the stuff laid out, just a nut or two and a sip at her drink. At first. But he was on to his second and sometimes his third and soon it got so that Bea was having to call dinner twice.

It upset the whole house. Mrs Pikes laying about her in the kitchen on account of the dinner always being held back and spoiled and May fed up with the sharp edge of her tongue. And Bea having to hang round in the passage outside the drawing room where it was always cold and the single oil lamp threw such weird shadows up the walls and snatched them back again in the draughts, you thought they were alive. She always got herself wrong-footed too, when the drawing-room door did finally open. Miss Camille sweeping out and turning in straight at the dining room. And Bea always pinned between the one door and the next, or the wall and the long oak chest. Caught in Brooksie's moustachioed smile, the warm fanning out of breath, alcohol-sharp and smoke-softened all at once. And the slippery, slurred words too low and quick for her ever to catch, though she knew their meaning. And the strong fingers, on her and gone before she could push them away.

But Miss Camille saw none of it. That was the time the light was never out of her eyes and her small mouth seemed always parted as if she was catching her breath.

*

The wedding of Donna Emilia and Duke Federico was celebrated before the month was out, on the feast of San Zenobio. Three days of dancing and masques and music, and La Pianta glittering from morning till night with the great families of the Veneto and beyond. Among them Federico moved, inclining his head this way and that, his thin lips curved in an unchanging smile. Federico was a man who did not care for society, except as a mirror for his own eminence. Except as a furtherance of those business transactions, that accumulation of possessions that were his passion.

But it was not the Duke who was the subject of the ceaseless buzz of conversation or the object – over shoulders, between heads, above the lace edges of fans – of every eye in the room. It was his Duchess. Every day a new dress and new and more opulent jewels that flamed up in the candlelight burning, each one, with fire at its heart. But the face above them reflected none of their glow. It held itself mask-like, taut with an almost childish stubbornness. Every day she appeared closely surrounded by her ladies, the shy, upland women with lowered eyes and broad hands she had brought with her from Malo. Wherever she moved they moved, like a school of minnows in a river, or a skein of geese in the sky. And late at night she was borne away again amidst the whispering hems of their dresses, as inviolate as a virgin queen.

During the lengthy feasts that were laid before her she ate almost nothing and though she lifted her gilded glass to every toast which required her response no-one ever saw the wine touch her lips. Only in dancing, sometimes, did she forget herself for a moment or two. And then it was like seeing a distant planet through a miraculously ground lens. All at once the planet's surface could be seen to leap with volcanic explosions, darken and crackle with thunderstorms, streak with lightning. It was not lost on the young blades – it was not lost on anyone present – the sudden flushing of her cheek, the harsh indrawing of her breath. They vied with each other to contrive to be opposite her as the dance required her to change partners, to take her hand, to lead her up the floor and see, perhaps, her cold eyes blaze for a second with this deep fire. To boast to each other later of how they had felt a magnetic charge leap from her finger ends. She saw that they talked of her, and how they looked at her. She knew herself watched by everyone. It was the reason, said some of the household servants to each other, that she held herself so stiff and unsmiling – all those eyes on her.

Then, by the morning of the fourth day they were gone, all of them. The dying flowers gone and the boughs of laurel, the guttered candles cleared from the candelabra and chandeliers. A sense of relief, of lightness lay about the emptied rooms along with the pale sunshine. There was in the house a quickness, an undercurrent of excitement and anticipation. Up in the secretariat we could not sit to our work; in the restless silence nibs broke and ink splattered. Below, trains of servants passing and repassing each other, weaving their way past knots of women scrubbing or polishing or sweeping with heavy brooms, would halt suddenly in their whispered conversations. Every time they crossed the hall they would glance up the stairs, towards the Duchess's apartments. As the day wore on and their tasks in the great rooms were completed, still they lingered, cloths hanging limply from their hands, brooms trailing ineffectually over the newly polished floorboards. Waiting.

And then, all at once, towards mid-afternoon, there she was, coming down the stairs in a green cape lined with marten's fur that billowed open with the movement of her descending and swirled around her feet as she paused for a moment before crossing the hall. She took them by surprise though their vigil had been for this precise moment. There was a swiftly broken-off murmuring like a wind rising and suddenly falling and in the silence the sense of the thronging of doorways. Those who happened to be already in the hall pressed themselves back against its walls dropping curtsies, bowing; yet it felt as though they pressed themselves forward to see. To touch. Like women in crowds who throng forward for a touch of the king's hand, or to touch for luck the condemned man as he walks to his gallows. As she moved towards the hastily flung-open door, as she passed between them, they saw close-to the whiteness of her neck, the softness of it where it fell into curves and lightly shadowed indentations. They breathed in the scent of her and stared at the coiled and braided hair, thick and dark, that glinted and shone in the light that streamed in from the doorway and knew how it might be loose and trailing over her shoulders, or overflowing from cupped hands, or like a fine-spun web moving after her over the lace of pillows. They stared at her and knew all this. They drank her in and she was reflected in all their eyes. They saw for themselves the fine pinch of her nostril, the delicately drawn mouth and the cushioned

fullness of her lower lip. But when they came to her eyes
they found them shuttered against them, veiled and cold;
a coldness that startled them and turned away their own
eyes. She did not smile. She did not nod to anyone.
Instead she drew her cloak about her and stepped out
into the garden followed closely by two of her women.
They heard the sound of footsteps receding over gravel.
And then the door was closed.

There was, for a moment, silence in the hall, stillness,
a sense of chill. Those who had craned their necks to see
the Duchess from adjoining passageways drew back and
then turned slowly away. And one by one the others
turned, all without speaking, so that there was just a
shuffling sound, a whispering of rough skirts against the
floor. It was with their eyes that they spoke to each other,
covertly, as practised servants do, until they reached the
safety of the kitchens. Then it was generally agreed,
with nods and smiles and the winking of eyes, that the
Duke had netted himself a beauty indeed. Indeed. But
there was something in that beauty that made some of
them shake their heads. And yet others turn away with
the coldness of the Duchess's eye chill as a lump of ice
in the pit of their stomachs.

Those who had felt a sense of foreboding at the naive
sweetness of the last Duchess's smile now felt the first
stirring of the same unease, but for the opposite reason.

If, during the days of her wedding, she had been the
focus of all attention, the subject of all conversations,
her every movement followed covertly or overtly by every
eye in that assembly of false smiles and busily working
tongues, now she became the magnetic centre of the
house. She was a scent on the stair, the muffled sound
of a lute. All those who could, found business to take
them up to her wing of the house. In the shadowed
passageway you could see dark forms loitering, listening.
Maids behind armfuls of linen, footmen with silver sal-
vers which might have borne letters or cups of warmed
wine, but which were always empty. Pages whose cheeks

flushed red and whose eyes were quickly averted whenever anyone encountered them there. Sometimes behind closed doors they heard singing: harsh, strident voices and the quick, broken rhythm of hands clapping, a strange, unfamiliar sound that enticed and frightened. Sometimes, in the long silences that followed, they thought they heard the low gasp of weeping. But not even the most cunning among them could prise information from her women. They were left with the debris of trays that were sent up to her rooms and the secrets of her linen. With the knowledge, never private in such large, inquisitive households, of when the Duke went to her and when he left her. They watched and they waited. They exchanged observation and anecdote, accumulating hearsay and detail, piling it up between kitchen and pantry and stableyard and laundry room.

It was noticed how she never ordered the white jennet given to her by the Duke to be saddled for excursions round the terraces of the garden. Nor was the carriage which he had put at her disposal ever brought at her command to the front door to drive out along the muddy roads. And yet whenever it was fine enough she could be seen walking in the gardens with one or more of her women, up one gravelled alley and down another, out to the very perimeter where the land had been artificially raised with rocks and boulders to look down over a diverted stream. Further than any lady should walk. Right out of sight of the house, sometimes. She could barely be seen by the eyes that watched from so many of the windows of La Pianta, no more than a dot of green in her cloak. They were always struck, those watchers, by how fast she strode over the gravel sweep away from the door of the house. Their suspicions, that once hidden by the yew hedges or a stand of trees – once out of sight of the house – she slowed her pace, were borne out by the evidence of the gardeners. She also, they said, stopped often and stared up for minutes at a time into the low sky beyond the desolate flatness of the winter fields to where the horizon was lost in greyness, gazing first in one direction and then another as though searching for something.

It was not lost on them. Pining, they said. Homesick. They tried, in their way, within the limits of their permitted informality with her, to draw her in to them. One smile, elicited at last from her, would make it easier for other smiles to follow. It was not right that such a young girl should hold herself so stiff. It was not wise to pine for hills when the Duke had brought her to live on the plain; it was not wise for anyone to set themselves against the Duke even in so natural a matter as a preference for one's homeland. Besides, it was not practical: whether she liked it or no she would spend the rest of her life at La Pianta. But they found her unmoveable. Intractable.

The head gardener, encountering her once during those early days and thinking to give her pleasure, pointed out to her where, high on a branch, delicate buds of winter blossom were unfurling. But her mouth only tightened, her brow creased and, after an uncertain pause, she swept on. The master of the stables, with young daughters of his own, begged leave to show her the new litter of puppies. Turning his hat nervously in his hands, he led the way down to the disused horsebox where the litter was. When he opened the door the puppies were sleeping, only the bitch stirred, she lifted her head and shifted her vast distended belly. The movement woke the pups who hurled themselves blindly to fasten again onto her reddened teats. Bartolomeo knelt to disengage one. 'Would your ladyship like to hold . . .' But even as he spoke, Bartolomeo recounted to the kitchen, she turned on her heel and stalked out, her ladies running awkwardly after her over the cobbles. 'And yet,' he mused, 'for a moment I saw in her eyes such a tender look . . .'

Bartolomeo's tale, repeated through the house, did not bring forth the smile, the rueful shake of the head of

other anecdotes. It elicited silence. It hushed the exuber-
ant gossip about her into anxious whispers. It admitted
the possibility that her behaviour was – deliberate.
There now came about a slight shift of attitude in the
house, as though they all took one step back from her.

*

Black hat, black gloves, black coat. Quick deliberate
steps. Like a raven scuttling between the trees. Everything else loses itself in the fog, but not Moira. Out into
the wide white meadow. Over the plank bridge. Fog rises
thick as a blanket over the stream. Up over the tree
roots and the criss-crossing paths. She knows it now by
heart.

Strange, close feeling in the wood today. Bushes loom
out of the fog at her. Trees stand like watchers almost
hidden by the mist. At the fork for Sladdacoombe she
doesn't turn, she doesn't even pause. On up she goes,
where the wood draws closer together. Where the path
darkens, hemmed in by a tangling of brambles and saplings, the broad, stubborn trunks of oaks and the dense
matted foliage of bushes. Moira's breathing drums loud
in her ears, the only sound. Is it? The only sound? She
strains to hear behind and to the side of her. She hurries
on, looking only before her. But her anxiety spreads out
all around her, a net of antennae listening, probing,
sweeping out over the rustling dead leaves, up through
the white stiffened air. And then suddenly the close trees
fall away. The mist tears slowly into shreds, hangs like
discarded scarves over bushes and she comes out on the
brow of Penbarrow Hill. The dark bulk of barns and
outhouses loom up to her right. She pauses, a black
shadow among the twisted shadows of the hawthorns
along the line of the hill. There's a gap in the trees
here, a scuffled path in the thin grass. It leads into the
farmyard. Davy's kingdom, Davy's province, the farmyard. Davy and she ... She knows another path. It

winds, narrow as a footstep along the back of the outhouses, sidles down between the dairy and the farmhouse
to the kitchen door. She slips quickly out of one shadow
into the other. Breathless when she rat-tats at the back
door.

'Oh, Moira!' Nan looks bemused, startled. 'I didn't
expect you round the back!' Like a young girl taken
unawares.

Moira steps in, over the threshold. Into the warm room.

'I got Jeth in bed.'

The smell of baking. Cakes set out to cool on a wire
tray. Cat asleep in an old armchair.

'Not well, is he?'

'Something he ate.' Nan, still distracted, picks up an
oven cloth, lifts open one of the small, heavy doors on the
kitchen range. 'Not like him. Got a cast-iron stomach.'

As she bends down to lift out loaves of bread a strand
of hair uncurls on the nape of her neck. On the white
skin between the heavy coil of her hair and the collar of
her jersey. Like a finger, beckoning. Moira takes off her
hat.

Moira always so smart. Just a velour, but still. Nan
puts the loaves on the table, one by one. Feels her face
hot from the stove, her body lumpy, heavy in its age, in
its sameness. Jumper and skirt, day after day. She'd had
a velour hat, once. Bottle green. When she first walked
out with Jeth, back in Finchampton. She'd kept up with
all the latest fashions then. She and her sisters and
Elspeth, her best friend. Ten shillings she'd given each
week to her mother and the rest was hers. They'd pored
over the fashion papers, plagued the local draper to order
them this and that. A green coat she'd had, too. Loden,
it had said in the catalogue. It hadn't quite matched the
hat, but still – loden – no-one else had one. Two shillings
a week the payments had been. That had been life, then.
Another life. A life of shops and market day and dances.
The packet of *papiers poudres* in her handbag with the
gilt chain, though her nose never seemed to get shiny

like Elspeth's. And the little pot of rouge hidden among her stockings at the back of her drawer, so her mother wouldn't find it. And the farmers' sons coming into Finchampton bold-eyed and soft as butter. Moira reminded her of those days. Moira'd lived a town life. You could see it.

Moira turns the brim of her hat slowly in her fingers. They aren't going to Long Sands now or Morne Bay. Not with Jeth ill. She feels ridiculous, overdressed. Out of place, here in this room. The half-light in the corners, the electric light on over the table, yellow, warm. Warm from the coal range and the drifting butter smell of the cakes and the sharp scent of the new bread. Beyond the long window the world is blotted out, swirled away. Whitened to nothing. Nothing but this room. And Nan.

'I'm sorry about Morne Bay and that,' says Nan, shutting the oven door. 'Still, we'll have tea here.' She smiles across the table, pink-cheeked from the fire, wiping her hands on the cloth so that her rings clink together. What was it about Moira reminds her . . . Reminds her – of someone. Someone in an office, long ago. Had strings of beads, bright scarves at her neck to match every outfit; smart, just like Moira. Poor Moira. Such things were lost on Sladdacoombe. Difficult making a change like that so late in life. Brave of her. And when you thought: first her mother, then her sister. 'We'll go another day, ' Nan says.

Moira puts down her hat on the window seat. On the faded chintz cushions. In among the piles of *Farming Weeklies* and mufflers and gloves and newspapers turned to crosswords and ball-point pens still clicked open. Like a black shadow it lies among all that soft-strewn clutter of lives. Along the windowsill between the pot plants a dusty blue feather, bits of coloured glass, a pipe with a polished walnut bowl and a roll of tobacco in waterproof. Nan's husband and Nan's son. Nan's life. All there. The room is full of it; it breathes it, pulses like warm blood with it. A life of home-made cake at teatime and a cat to have on your knee. And in the summer it would be all bowling along roads between green hills, alongside the flash of sea. Off out. Every day. She turns from the window.

'We'll have to learn to drive,' she says.

Nan laughs.

Pretty Nan, always laughing; smiles come quick to her lips, second nature for them. She'd be pretty, she'd laugh, too, in a room like this – house like this – life . . .

*

It was one Thursday in early June, a heavy sultry day, that Bernard, up in his signal box at the Pont St Honore halt saw Jean-Luc come for the midday train. Even in shirtsleeves, Bernard, working his levers, had sweat running down his back and trickling from his forehead; but Jean-Luc was trussed up in a black suit that looked as if it lay on him heavy as serge, with a cravat tying the thick shirt collar tight to his neck. He stood uneasily in the cinders at the side of the track with a small valise, staring straight ahead of him. Bernard, unable to leave the box because of the approaching train, could not even discover from him where he was going. In the village, lifeless in the noontide heat, nothing stirred, so that not even the roaming dogs or the small boys came to stare, and his departure went unnoticed.

He did not return that evening or the next day.

But the dog was still tied to the steps of his front porch. And the ferrets still ran snarling and chittering in their long runs. And the dead birds still turned slowly on the wire.

The following day, towards mid-afternoon, the stopping train from Amiens drew to a halt at Pont St Honore. Two people got down, only their feet visible between the wheels of the carriages. When the train pulled slowly away again in a cloud of smoke that billowed out over the water meadows there was Jean-Luc. With a woman on his arm. They stood in the white glare of sunlight without moving, as if they were caught in a photographer's flare, dazed for the minute. The barrier was pushed, creaking, back off the road. The signal arm dropped with a clatter of weariness and in the returning silence the rails hummed faintly with the whisper of the departed train. And there was nothing else for it but to walk forward. Jean-Luc, with his fool's grin crept over his face, looked down at the dust on his boots. While she, clutching tighter at the strings of her felt-work bag, lifted her chin bravely in the air. On the empty afternoon road her foot came down spraying gravel at each step like glass splintering. And following after, quick though she was, practised, came the dead sound of something dragged. Beneath the brown skirt that trailed in the dust nothing could be seen. And nothing seen in her face either, a sallow face, long-nosed and long-jawed. Only the small feather curled on her hat trembled.

Over the railway tracks and past the first low cottages and the thin-faced houses with their dark, slatted wooden shutters. On between the double line of armless plane trees, till the houses stop and the mutilated trees and the gravel road peters out into grass. And the track begins. And nothing to be seen but the curious dipping roll to her hips as she walked, lower to one side than the other, and behind her, deeply scored in the gravel, the marks like semaphore-tracing. But from behind the darkness of windows and the shadows of open doorways they saw, they saw everything.

We saw her too. The blue feather on the little blue hat bobbing up and down above the reed. We paused in our digging a minute or two and watched them. Her hand was not on his arm any longer but she kept up within a pace of two of him, her head bent to the ruts in the road. No doubt the track rougher than she had expected and the way further from the village than she had thought it would be. We saw them come clear of the reed, out into the open space before the dunes and watched them down to where the track ends. We thought at first she stumbled as she walked, tripping in the muddy holes and the soft, slippery places. And then as the curious movement continued that, perhaps, she danced – we saw how she lifted her skirts to her ankles. It did not strike us then, or perhaps we were just too far to see, the difference between her black buttoned boots; the heaviness of the one against the lightness of the other. We saw how the dog leaped and barked at the end of its rope at their approach. How it did not cringe away as Jean-Luc neared the porch steps, but wagged its tail and licked at their knees. And how for once Jean-Luc did not kick it aside. We saw him open the door for the woman and incline his head. And we saw her pass inside.

The story was soon out, though it did not reach our ears for several days. But by the end of that first night we had grasped the essence of it. Leon, at the sight of the woman, became as excitable as if he had glimpsed some rare migratory visitor to the marsh. For the rest of the afternoon he looked up constantly with sudden sharp movements of his head as if she might escape back up the track to Pont St Honore without his catching sight of her again. Attempts to keep him at home that evening were in vain. When he returned, however, he was silent. Bemused. He did not caper on the hearthrug or parade across the floor, He sat at the table opposite me where I was cleaning the parts of an old oil lamp. Wide-eyed. Watching me. And then very slowly he lifted one hand and, curling back the fingers, all except the third, to hide them from me in his palm, began to turn the finger this way and that. He stared at it, a small foolish smile softening his mouth; the smile, to the life, of a young woman who thinks herself unobserved. I let the rag lie still on the rusty wick-holder and watched him. He rolled something invisible round on the finger, slid it slowly up over the joint and down again. Leaned across to where the lamp stood on the end of the table and held it under the pool of light. He twirled the finger, moving it close to the globe of the lamp and drawing it back sharply again, his eyes never leaving it.

'Well,' I said, 'married!'

He passed his right hand over his left, covering it with the stately gesture of a magician concluding a demonstration.

'You go and knock on their door, offer your felicitations, then?'

Leon flung back his chair, his eyes almost closed in their rage and hurled himself out of the room.

Through a matrimonial journal it had been, we heard: *Union des Familles, Monde Familiale* – some such thing. It was not unknown, not unusual. In remote places. Districts where there was no matchmaker. Up in Pont St Honore, behind their dark watchful eyes, out of their expressionless faces, they laughed. Like the sharp teeth of the fox behind the amiable grin of its muzzle. Jean-Luc was reticent; as well, they said, he might be. But she . . . She had blushed as she had coyly admitted they had met through the pages of a journal. Not the reddening of her cheeks for shame, but a soft glow of pink, as though at a romantic memory. She had smiled at them as she spoke. They had seen that smile before – the confessional smile of the newly betrothed. They watched her limp away down the street.

From Amiens, she was. Strange, in a big place like that, they said, she couldn't have found herself a sweetheart. Strange she should want to bury herself miles from anywhere when she wasn't bred to it, for all she said she'd always wanted to live by the sea, never cared for the life of towns. A haberdasher's assistant she'd been. You could see that, all those matching buttons and twists of ribbon here and there and that fancy braid along the bottoms of her skirts. Wouldn't last long in old Marsat's shack. Lived with her sister's family. Very particular her brother-in-law had been, she said, advising her against several would-be suitors who had written to her. Particular! they repeated behind her retreating back. Particular hurry, more like! Particular haste to get rid of her while she was still of marriageable age. And which had been in the most haste, the brother-in-law? Or the sister? And if Jean-Luc had been the best of the bunch, what had the rest been like!

The wagtail dances before his bride, a quick flashing of light and dark at the muddy edges of pools; a spreading out of his wing feathers in exaggerated display and a quick gathering up again, bobbing in quarter turns each to the other. The frog puffs out his throat, distends it till it is a vast swelling and from its engorgement croons all night long to his lady-love crouching in the reeds. And the lapwings drop through the air, folded wing to wing around each other. But their courtship had been all by letter. Words laid out in display before each other. And words hid away. Blurred photographs. And agreement come to before they even set eyes on each other. The bargain set. And pride, or honour – or desperation – such that she did not recoil when Jean-Luc presented himself at the door of her sister's house. Or could not.

If there was concealment, then the one paid off the other, they said in Pont St Honore.

The days passed but it soon became clear to us that nothing she found in her new home was quite as she'd bargained.

Invisible to her no doubt we were. After so many years we had come to take on the aspect of the marsh itself, neither of us much taller than the reed at its full summer height, bowed slightly, stooped, and little to distinguish us from the colour of the marsh; our clothes seeming as old as ourselves. But we could not help but take heed of her. It was as though she was in a lighted space in the dark of the bending reed. A beacon that drew our eyes.

We saw her sweep sand off the porch each morning, her sleeves rolled to the elbows. We saw her pump water at the side of the house, the lean of her body against the rusted handle and the twisting sparkle of water in air as gout after gout spurted from the mouth of the pump. We saw how the wind tore tendrils of hair loose from the knot at the back of her neck, whipping them across her forehead and cheeks. How her skirt blustered and wrapped itself round her ankles, hobbling her. Or streamed flapping behind her, cracking like a loose sail, unbalancing her. There was always wind on the marsh. We were used to it. It was for us a kind of daily journal. We put our heads up to it and read in it what was to come: the varying scents carried on it, its veering and rising and dropping, they all had meaning and portent for us. But we saw how it plagued her, the unceasingness of it. The wilfulness of it – the fire blown out in the range, the sand blown back up the steps. No doubt it had not entered into her conjectures about her new life. No doubt none of what she found compared.

One afternoon she brought a chair out onto the porch and a pile of mending, but the wind lifted the material clear off her lap and scattered the pins to the floor. We heard the little tin box crash and roll over and over like the high clear note of a small bell and the shower of pins falling against each other echo over the marsh.

We watched her climb the sand-dunes behind the house, hauling herself up from tuft to tuft of the wiry grass that clung there. Stumbling and swaying in the soft avalanches of sand as she reached the crest and then disappearing down onto the beach. But always the wind drove her back. No-one could stay on Belle Plage for long. *Purgatoire* they called it in St Honore. The incessant shrieking and whistling of the wind, the torment of the sand that stung you and the pebbles that ran knocking at your heels.

Sometimes she walked out into the marsh. We saw posies of water purslane and St John's wort in her hands. We saw her stand, watching the water birds. And we saw, too, how she would suddenly stop and turn and look around her on all sides. As though she heard something.

As though she sensed something. Perhaps the quake pressed too close; in some parts it took the main path away for a step or two, softening it to water. Perhaps she became afraid. But always she would go back at this point, her head bent, her step slower and more laboured. And coming out where the reed fell away, where the path met the gravelled space before the house, she would pause. She would pause and then with a reluctance, with a finality, would come her quiet footsteps unevenly over the gravel, reverberating over the planks of the porch. We would hear the creak of the door and the sharp drop of its iron latch into the lock behind her.

Autumn slid into winter early that year with days that clustered together hard and sparkling, bound by a rim of frost under an arch of sky as blue and clear as blown glass. Days that might shatter at a touch, at the slightest carelessness, where every movement the Duchess made had a dark shadow following it across the white-washed walls of her rooms. And lost, uncertain days. Days when thick grey fogs curled around La Pianta pressing in and shutting out the light, removing it from the familiar world to a world of stifled silence. Days when the Duchess saw the sun only fleetingly as the fog tore itself apart in smoky fragments revealing a sun as small and white as a moon. It seemed to filter invisibly through cracks at windows and around doors, filling rooms with its dead, ash-like taste, lying along the skirtings of corridors and twisting down staircases. Maids held their aprons to their faces against its acrid scent and the rheums and agues it brought with it.

But Tomaso, a lawn handkerchief at his nose, glided more silently than ever around the darkened passages of La Pianta. He paused, listening, at doorways and eavesdropped on gossiping servant-girls in the labyrinth of narrow corridors below stairs. He sat in his little shuttered room and had intelligences brought to him. They talked, all of them, of the Duchess. Even those who came to him in secret and watched his face as they told their tales, trying to guess what it was he wanted to hear.

The Duchess was a spy. She had been observed on

Thursday last to receive another packet of letters from the north.

She was a witch.

She did again, last afternoon, sit at dinner without speaking once to her lord except to answer his questions. She did, in a manner that seemed to have some purpose in it, refuse all delicacies that were offered to her, picking only at the plainest food.

The shadows crouched and leaped against the wall and Tomaso laughed silently. Petty crimes, all of them, yet they would do, they would suffice. His eyes were almost closed as he licked his forefinger and, stretching out his hand, pinched the wick of the candle with finger and thumb. With a startled hiss the flame was extinguished. Tomaso liked the sudden smell of candle wax that followed, the white curling tongue of smoke, the darkness that fell like a soft cloak around him.

He thought of the Duke's thin cold fingers on the warm body of the Duchess running quickly, touching, scrabbling at her. And the long tongue ceaselessly moving, searching her out, devouring her. She did not resist him, he knew that from the evidence of the laundresses. Yet – there was something. Something that she . . . What? What was it kept her women still tight-lipped and anxious? What was it that they heard? What was it that they saw? It was time he contrived to have them sent home, these women, so that he could put his own people in place. So that he could know everything. So that he could witness at second-hand – or even at first . . . He was, after all, the Duke's private secretary. In the whole household he was the man closest to the Duke, almost his confidant. Almost, he whispered, almost.

He could feel it coming, feel the need leaching out of Federico and being drawn back in again. The Duke had called for him after midnight the other night, had had him woken, on little more than a pretext.

'I wish to hasten this deal with the Admanti,' he had

said, clutching at the edges of his robe, kneading the soft fur. 'Only if we move quickly can we have the advantage!'

It was there again, Tomaso had noticed, the drowsiness slipping off him as he watched, that convulsive move-ment of the fingers, the need to hold things: the papers that lay before him, the arm of his chair, the sleeve of his coat. The need to touch and feel reassured by the certainty of solid form. A movement so slight, so — expected — among the gestures of other men that only Tomaso noticed it was alien to Federico. In the locked drawer of Tomaso's table in the secretariat, to which only he and the Duke had a key, he found each morning a larger sheaf of memoranda from Federico. Memoranda which had not been there when he had closed his desk for the night, notes for new projects, projects all of acqui-sition: trading companies, land, people, works of art. The night thoughts of the Duke of Piacenza e Lusia. And all of possession. A sated man, Tomaso mused, a sated man would have no need . . .

He rose and left his room and, padding silently through the passageways, began to climb the back stairs. Near the top he met one of the younger pages.

'Where's Filippo?'

'With the Duke, sir.'

Filippo had preferment now, kept always at the Duke's side. Yet, from the way he appeared to hang inert and pale behind the Duke's chair, he seemed to have little joy of it. It was a rare preferment, such as the household could not remember before, for after some time he was ordered to move his truckle bed out of the pages' dormi-tory and into the small anteroom beside the Duke's bed-chamber where his valet slept. So that he could be called on by His Grace at any hour, it was thought. The Duke was much taken up, it was said, with business late into the night. Despite his new wife. And Filippo, by the look of him, was kept up with him. They teased him for the dark circles that began to shadow his eyes, the tenseness that haunted his face, the way he jumped at the slightest untoward sound. But he did not laugh with them. He looked back at them from such an unfathomable distance, almost as though he did not recognise them or understand the meaning of what they said. He seemed to stare into some private preoccupation and so, eventually, they left him alone with it.

It was not only Tomaso who noticed how Filippo's preferment was little more than that of a chained dog. Federico kept him with him constantly and yet, to those who watched closely, it became clear that even the sight of the boy had begun to enrage the Duke. It was carefully hidden. Federico had made it always a practice never to allow the slightest element of advantage to present itself to those who might be his enemies. The sudden swivelling of his head in Filippo's direction would seem to a casual observer no more than the usual peremptoriness. The glimpse, as he turned, of the pale flecked eyes closed and curiously blind, gave no hint of their brief malevolence – except to those who watched Filippo. Then you could see how Filippo's own eyes widened in fear as the Duke's head whipped round in his direction and then snapped back. Filippo diligently observed all the forms of courtesy and obeisance whenever the Duke, with barely detectable unwillingness, ordered him to perform some task but you saw that the more Filippo bowed the more Federico distrusted him.

Now when Tomaso passed the boy in the corridor Filippo would turn to him and halt, so obviously lost in perplexity or beset with fear, that he looked as though he was about to speak to him openly of the matter and Tomaso would hurry on to prevent it. He had planted the seed and it had grown, fed by silence – the proud silence of the Duke and the terrified silence of Filippo – and warmed, in the absence of the sun, by the feverish heat of jealousy.

Tomaso turned left and then left again into the familiar corridor. The sun. He leaned against the door jamb of the Duchess's apartment and rapped sharply against

the door with the knuckle of his index finger. Without
the sun nothing would have grown. The door was opened
part-way and then the woman, recognising who it was,
stood back. He was not welcome here, he knew that,
but he knew also that they dared not refuse him entry.
Tomaso did not address the woman, he did not even
bother to nod his head. She led him through into the
inner sitting room. The Duchess, standing by one of the
long windows, turned slowly, unsmilingly. Ah, just so
madam, Tomaso whispered in his head, taking in the icy
blankness of her stare, the slight, derisive downward
droop of the outer corners of her mouth. Just so. When
we are not shown the face of the sun that we expect,
when we are shown a cold face, though we know the sun
is hot, why then we suppose the sun shows its hot face
to another.

'Good morning, madam.'

'What is good about it, Master Secretary? It rains
again.'

She was bold, she held his eyes from the moment he
glanced up at her.

'Good for the fields, madam.' He moved swiftly across
the room, never lowering his eyes from hers.

'I did not know you added farming to your – many –
talents.'

'All that concerns La Pianta concerns me,' he paused
momentarily, 'madam. I trust that by now you think of
La Pianta as your home.' She turned away sharply, back
to the window, with a little hiss of breath. He came
closer to her cutting her off from the women who hovered
anxiously against the far wall. 'The Duke would have it
so; he expects it of you, madam. He would not wish to
take your – memories of home – from you,' he glanced
at her serving women and then quickly back to the Duchess, 'but add to them with new delights.' He thought he
saw, reflected in the glass, that momentarily she closed
her eyes.

Every day he came with some new excuse, some new

invention; some new solicitude. The upstairs maids laughed and said he was enamoured of her, but close observance of Tomaso's face would have told them that this was not so. Every day he forced himself upon her and watched how she recoiled in distaste. It took very little pressure, very little and there she was, her back against a wall, for she could not refuse him entrance. He tried her and saw each time how limited was her response. It lay simply in the withholding of herself, a trick she had of, though physically being present, holding herself absent, apart. Perhaps she thought it a covert game, a misdemeanour about which no evidence could be brought to accuse her. If so, she had reckoned without the power of the Duke, who needed neither evidence nor justification.

Tomaso crossed the room slowly; at the table on which her tame finch sat he paused as if remembering something and ran his fingernail lightly across the gilt bars. The bird fluttered in alarm.

'There is some new lute music, madam, sent among other things today from Venice. I will have it brought to you directly.'

'Do not trouble yourself, Master Secretary.'

'It is no trouble, madam.' He turned at the door. 'They are all – duets: I will send Filippo to you with them.'

Filippo was indeed sent, towards the end of that very afternoon. But he was not given admittance to the Duchess's apartments. A maid taking some last thing up to the suite of rooms prepared for the imminent arrival of the Duke's sister saw him, a lute drooping from one hand, a sheaf of papers quivering in the other. She stood in a doorway to watch unnoticed. She heard him plead with the woman who barred his way, his voice rising in despair and falling again, though she could not catch the words. She saw his body curve and writhe as though in anguish.

'He pressed his suit so fervently,' she reported below

112

stairs, 'you would have thought the torments of hell were waiting for him should he fail. But still the woman shook her head. And still he pressed the papers on her until at last she took them and shut the door on him. Yet even then he did not go. He stood there fingering the neck of the lute, staring at the door, edging away a few paces, glancing behind him into the shadows of the corridor. Finally, uneasily, sideways like a crab, he sidled off into the darkness.'

*

Jean-Luc set himself to build more runs for his ferrets. Around the house a ramshackle patchwork of cages sprang up knocked together out of driftwood and old packing cases and planks dismantled from the remains of Marsat's shed. The dog whined and tugged on its rope and paced disconsolate in and out of the shadow of the porch as Jean-Luc put the ferrets to their new quarters. One by one he took them up, his hands closing tight around them, holding them close. White they were against his coat, only their heads free. He bent his face to them, crooning at them, stroking them. Some held themselves quiet in his hands, sharp-nosed and glint-eyed, their little ears prickling and lying down again at each new sound. But others, sensing the free air beyond the imprisoning fingers, twisted and turned, chattering in their rage, baring their teeth to bite their way out of this new cage. But Jean-Luc would only laugh and hold them tighter, his own lips drawn back over his teeth as he watched their hopeless struggle. When they were all put away he turned to a sack on the ground, tied at its mouth, that seemed to wriggle and heave. He gave it a kick with his foot and it lay still. He untied the string and put his foot on the neck of the sack to keep it closed.

'Laurette!' he called. And again. Four times he had to call her name and a black look came over his face.

She came at last, hobbling down the steps, and it seemed to us as though she was slower than before.

'What is it?' She halted, one hand steadying herself against the struts of the porch.

The grin slid quickly along his mouth again and narrowed his eyes. He jerked his head towards the pens.

'. . . show you.'

She limped towards him, over the sand. He waited till she was up close and then, kicking his foot clear of the sack, bending down and sliding his hand in, drawing it out again and stamping the neck of the sack shut so quick it looked all one movement, he held up his hand before her with a young rabbit dangling by its ears. It hung there, stunned with terror. We saw her mouth open as if in a gasp, saw her lift her arms towards the creature. But Jean-Luc's free hand pounced on her, gripping her wrist, holding her back. It was evident that he had not latched the trapdoor in the netting roof of the nearest cage for he now leant down, pulling her with him, to knock it open with the side of his hand, drop in the rabbit and slam it shut again. Before the rabbit's scream we heard her cry. We saw her wrestle with him over the top of the cage, her tight little fists raised against the sky. She struggled free and he laughed as he caught her again, holding her now hard against him. He darted kisses at her and we saw how she tossed her head from side to side, lowered it and, as he lowered his, flung it back in despair. She beat at him with her hands and pushed at his shoulders. But he only straddled his legs more firmly in the sand as they swayed there together. The rabbit's scream gurgled into silence and he bent his head to her and began biting her. Up and down her arms, over her shoulders and her neck, growling in his throat. And she leaping wilder than before. High, anguished cries he tore out of her, razor sharp, cutting the air. Around us fowl took to the wing in fright.

And we, we turned away our heads.

114

Not a word of it did she speak. Not of the life that she found herself in, nor the man that she had wedded. They waited up in Pont St Honore; they knew the man, they knew the marsh and the house that none of them would live in. But she said nothing. Not a word. Only to her letters.

We were in Madame Bouride's when she brought the first. We entered and saw her before us at the counter, almost lost in the shadows cast by the dark shelves that hung like caves all the way up to the ceiling. We stood by the door in a patch of sunlight that lay across the floor, Leon, behind me, trying to press himself into invisibility beside the net of carbolic soap. In the silence we watched the long, stained blade of Madame Bouride's knife as she pressed it down through a piece of cheese. Fragments crumbled and, as the knife bit deeper, a lump leaned slowly out from the larger piece of cheese, wobbled and fell, breaking in two. Madame Bouride placed it on a small square of brown paper and pushed it towards Laurette's other purchases with the tips of her fingers. It was her habit to make no more exertion than she was forced to, nor to speak more than the necessary words. It gave to her a look of stone and her words, when they came, were hard and cold as iron.

We saw how she discomfited Laurette, practised though she was in the art of shop dealings, expecting as she might to derive some pleasure from being now the customer instead of the shop assistant. We heard the brightness in her voice waver. And as she bent her head to her purse, searching among the centimes, so Madame Bouride lifted hers, with a fleeting glint of satisfaction in her eyes. But Laurette did not pick up her provisions, murmur good-day to each of us and shuffle out into the street. From the bottom of her basket, which we had thought empty, she drew an envelope. Small and almost square it was, with a bluish tinge to it, yet it flashed in that shadowy gloom as though it was gold or diamonds.

'I have a letter . . .'

Madame Bouride, dropping francs and centimes into their appointed places in the deep drawer below the counter, lifted her head sharply. Her hand still hovered over the open drawer, but we could see briefly in her eyes how her whole energy was drawn to that glimmering bluish-white square of folded paper.

'. . . but I can't find a postbox.'

'You give it here.'

'Here?'

'To me.'

'You – take the letters, madame?'

It was as if she had glimpsed already the kettle that waited on the hob in the back room, the blunt-edged paper knife and the pot of cow's-foot glue beside it. But Madame Bouride, puffed like a toad, did not speak further. She waited – for the envelope to be placed before her, to be put down on the scratched wooden surface of the counter. To be given over, into her charge. And by the door we waited too. We saw how Laurette hesitated and then, because there was no help for it, nothing else she knew to do, how slowly she put the letter down in front of Madame Bouride; gently, as if it was made of glass. There were people in Pont St Honore who would walk to Marie les Bains or even as far as Epay, rather than give over a letter for posting to Madame Bouride. We stared at the envelope lying defenceless before her and, behind me, I felt Leon shrink further back into the wall. Glass it might as well have been. Transparent. By that evening Evangeline Bouride would know all there was to know.

*

March passed. And April too. And then it was May. Bea couldn't believe the warmth there was all of a sudden in the air. She had to keep poking her head out of doors, to feel it. To make sure. Something had gone out of the air she said: something iron and hard, something strung tight. Now it was so soft you almost fell into it; so light you were buoyed up. It was like a conjuring trick.

They laughed at her in the kitchen.

'Spring always comes, our Bea,' said Mrs Pikes kneading bread at the long table.

It was funny that Miss Camille should go down with a cold just when the weather had turned so warm. Quite poorly she was, had to stay in bed for almost a week. He was always off to Kendal for grapes for her or hothouse roses. Away all morning, right up to lunch. You couldn't blame him, said Bea, such lovely weather. And yet you felt something inside him, an eagerness, that leaped up. Like a man contained for too long. It scared her, she said, the strength of it. If she could see it, she thought, Miss Camille must too. But he was too clever for that.

Every afternoon after lunch he'd follow Bea with the coffee tray up to Miss Camille's room, carrying his little present; turning on the charm, laying himself out for her. He knew how to give himself. It was a trick he had, a gift. He knew how to focus every speck of his attention on you, how to glow like the sun. So that you were warmed and dazzled, so you saw nothing else but him. And he had all of you. He wouldn't let her slide off into a corner of her mind where she had some preoccupation. He'd have it out of her in a second and she wouldn't be able to deny him. He made her believe he thought she was the Queen of Sheba, sitting there in her lilac bedjacket with the rows of lace and her face the colour of yesterday's porridge and her eyes hollowed shadows and her voice no more than a wheeze.

He started going out after tea as well. Sometimes he'd gone by the time Bea came up to take down the tray at half past five. Sometimes he was just on his way out.

'Off for my constitutional!' he would say. And Miss Camille would smile from her pillows, her eyes already closed.

Once when Bea came up for the tray, the bedroom door was ajar. She couldn't help but see in. Looking straight into the dressing-table mirror she was, one of those three-sided winged mirrors and the light coming in right behind it.

'Lovely evening, Camy,' she heard him say from somewhere in the room, his voice warm and slow.

'Mmm.' Miss Camille sounded like she'd already nodded off.

'Lovely light over the hills and the sheep all coming home . . .'

Bea lifted her hand to knock. And at the same moment a blurred shape moved in the mirror and, coming quickly from behind it, a hand. A soft white hand with stretching, probing fingers. And then another hand. Like blinded, wriggling worms, they were. But knowing. Silent. Behind the door Bea didn't dare move, she didn't dare hardly breathe. Up in the air the fingers stretched, little plump pads on the ends of them reflected clearly, then down, out towards the mirror, nearer and nearer as though any minute they would touch it and overtopple it. And then they were still. For a moment. Hanging, the fingers of one hand; draped almost, over something shadowed by the curtain. Something dark and square. The fingers flexed and something slid towards them in the mirror. Light wood and dark wood and a black space in between. The fingers slid inside and darted out again so quick Bea wasn't even sure she'd seen them. They rested on the edge of the wood and the dark space telescoped itself away. Down the fingers went, slithering and pressing themselves against the wood of the Wellington chest, counting off the narrow little drawers. At the fourth they paused again and flexed again and the dark space opened up once more for them. This time, however, they found their prey. Bea saw them drop on it and struggle with it. It got lifted up momentarily, flapping white, as the fingers engulfed it, folding it smaller and smaller until the five-pound note vanished inside the hand. It all went still in the mirror. The hand holding the note dropped out of sight. The other hand pushed the drawer closed, feeling with the tips of its fingers that the join was perfect.

'See you in a jiffy, old girl,' murmured Mr Brookes's voice.

Bea heard his footsteps creak across the room towards her. And where, before, she had been frozen stiff with fright, now everything jumped up and down inside her, thudding and pounding, her heart racing and her head dizzy and nothing obeying her. She pushed her hand at the door before he could discover her behind it, but it would not make an ordered knock, just a scrabbling sound against the polished panels. As the door swung slowly open she stumbled through it. All she could think of, she said, was not being found in the corridor. And then, of course, all she could think of was having pushed in front of Mr Brookes. But he was already gone, without so much as even seeming to notice her.

He got later and later back from these jaunts. She started asking where he was. And it was Bea had to tell her. Sunset it was. And then dark.

'Still out, ma'am.'

'Walking? This late?'

'In the car, ma'am.'

She was up and about again within the week. And he was dancing attendance on her like before. Only quicker. Double time. Doing a real fandango with shawls and cardigans and leaping up and down at imaginary draughts. Calling all the time for the fire to be built up, only whatever you did to it it still looked pale and wan in all that sunshine. And then as soon as Bea added more logs, whisking Miss Camille off out again. Drives and teas and whatever else.

They all went along with it, smiling and opening doors and saying 'Yes sir,' 'No sir,' and telling each other how much better the mistress was looking. But underneath, Bea said, you could feel the edge. You could feel a kind of space, a waiting for what they knew was coming. A silence where they none of them were saying anything.

He didn't keep them waiting long. Bea heard him one morning close to midday, from the kitchen. His whistle, startling and clear as if it had been a signal, in the hall. The scrape and rhythmic whirring of the crank handle. And the sudden cough of the car's engine. But each as a separate sound without connectedness, nothing piercing her daydream where she sat in a patch of sunlight. Not till the gunshot clatter of gravel came and the car engine roared up and trailed away to an echo out on the road.

'They're not going out *now*, it's nearly lunch!' Mrs Pikes threw down the apple she was slicing into a pie dish.

But the silence was already dropping down with the dust, falling back to fill up the spaces where they had been. You could almost hear it settling, thick, like snow in the empty rooms.

'Car's gone,' whispered May.

Bea shivered. Cold, she felt, in the pit of her stomach, an anxiousness knotting and weaving like fingers playing cat's cradle. Out in the passage, she could hear the swinging of the service door behind her all the way to the hall. Like it was swinging on its own accord, mocking her. And all the house felt queer; close around her, like it wasn't empty. The coloured light on the floor from the glass in the hall eerie. And the open doors she passed not giving on to nothing. She kept on glancing sharply over her shoulder. 'There's no-one here,' she kept saying to herself. 'There's no-one here.' So when she came to the drawing-room door, she couldn't let herself knock. Scared as she was.

Bea swore the room was empty when she looked first. The door swung open and there it was, chair by chair and all of it flat and washed-out looking, like it always was in the late mornings. She even heard her breath rush out in a sigh of relief. And then there she was, Miss Camille, in a chair. Only not like Miss Camille, not like a person, but a picture cut out of thin paper and coloured in faded, washed-out colours, pale as the room, her head turned, though Bea had caught no movement, and looking at Bea. And Bea staring at her. She caught herself up at once.

'Oh, Miss!' she gasped, quite forgetting. 'I – I come about the fire.'

Miss Camille stirred in her chair, she lifted her hand and the paperiness of her turned back again into flesh and bone.

'It's far too hot for fires, Bea,' she replied. 'I think no more fires, unless it gets very cold perhaps, in the evenings.'

'Very good, ma'am. Sorry to have bothered you ma'am . . . and not knocking . . . only I thought – I thought you'd gone out . . .'

'That's Mr Brookes, gone off for his morning constitutional.' She wrinkled up her nose, the way she had, to make you think it was all such a joke. 'Gone to see a man about a dog!' And she grinned.

'Yes, ma'am.'

'I warned him we wouldn't wait lunch.'

'Dog!' Mrs Pikes snorted, her knife going chop-chop more vicious than ever among the green beans. 'Two-legged dog. Dog with a skirt on!'

'And there are to be no more fires,' said Bea, stern as she could. 'And we're not to wait lunch.'

May caught at her arm as she passed, her face all lit up.

'A puppy?'

Bea nodded.

But he didn't come back with no dog, Not that day or the next. And the one after that he missed lunch altogether.

They didn't row, Bea said, not that you could hear. And there was in all the house now a listening, an uncertainty. A pattern broken and anxiety about how it would be re-made. Miss Camille was stiff with him for a couple of days. But he got her round. All dog-eyes and wagging his tail fit to bust. And jaunty. Like he knew he wouldn't lose.

'She's got the purse-strings!' exclaimed Mrs Pikes. 'Why doesn't she use them?'

But he could have out-manoeuvred her anywhere. It didn't take much to see that. And when the dust settled and the days dragged out again, long, with the light staying later, there they were. But different. Like they had masks on. And their voices different, coming through the mask. And what they said.

It was only what everyone said. It was only what you could have heard in every parlour up and down the land and in every hallway. Or repeated, in the way that every-thing heard was repeated, below stairs in every house. People long married. Half of them never been in love with each other to start with and the other half lost interest. That's how it was all over. Women with nothing much in their lives to fill up the day but lunches and teas and bridge and doing flowers. Busy, they said they were. Rushed off their feet. And the men that left them to it. Preoccupied with business they were supposed to be, only it was sitting about in clubs half the night rather than at home with their wives, or off out with the boys. All excuses. All pretend. Papering over the cracks. Rush-ing about with blindfolds over their heads and scraps of paper in one hand and a gluepot in the other, screeching and chattering all the time to distract attention. They all come to it in the end. But Bea got herself upset. She didn't want that for her Miss Camille.

They started talking lies, she said. And calling each other Mr Brookes and Mrs Brookes, like they were strangers. Like it was a joke. And laughing a lot in new, hard, bright voices. Only it wasn't a joke. You could feel a space widening between them. And their movements getting jerky, like the mask wasn't only over their faces, but down over their bodies, too. Like they weren't easy with each other any more. Like they couldn't sit still. Him especially.

He'd started going off again, leaving her alone. First it was just an hour now and then in the late morning, then it was two. Then it was every day, regular as clockwork. Off to the public house at Grange, he said.

'You wouldn't like it. It's just benches set round the walls of the front room of a cottage full of the foulest-smelling pipe smoke I've come across and the oldest farmers' lads since Methuselah.' He tried to wrinkle his nose up the way she did. 'And there aren't any salted nuts.'

But she didn't smile.

Then he started slipping off in the afternoons, too, like when she was ill. All of a sudden he had letters that had to catch the last post for London. Or he found he'd run out of cigarettes. Once Bea heard her argue back.

'Didn't we get some when we were in Kendal the other day?'

But he didn't turn a hair.

'There's not a gasper left, old girl. Hunted high and low after lunch. We must have smoked them all.' And he'd wink. 'We'll have to stop!'

And soon she fell silent. If he wanted to go, how could she stop him? She couldn't chain him.

Little by little Miss Camille started to repeat his excuses as if they were real. Echoing him phrase for phrase, only turned around. Bea'd hear it one way from him if she passed him in the hall or on the stairs as he was slipping out. And then another way from her, later.

'Mountain of things to do this morning, Bea,' she'd say with her new sharp laugh that sounded more and more like a high-pitched gasp of pain. 'Glad to get Mr Brookes out from under my feet!'

'Yes ma'am,' Bea would mutter, scurrying round straightening the chairs and plumping up the cushions and finishing off among the knick-knacks with her feather duster quick as she could to get out of the room. Anything not to have to see Miss Camille, sitting ramrod straight and still in front of the bureau, staring out at the wet lawn. She had nothing, Miss Camille. Only him. She'd done it all for him. Left London. Gone up there where she didn't seem to know a soul. All for him.

He got very light of foot, Bea said. Creepy. So that you never knew where you might come across him in the house. Always ferreting about upstairs when Miss Camille was downstairs. Always coming out of rooms where, to her mind, he had no business. Slipping out sideways, like through a crack in the wall. Closing the door very quietly, watching the handle with an almost listening stare as he slowly turned the knob so there was just a hushed squeak as it shut. Then, when he looked up and saw you, the slippery smile was spread quick as lightning over his face and the carefulness dropped so fast you had to pinch yourself. Bea couldn't help but think of the fingers in the mirror and the note being folded and folded away into nothing. They were practised, those fingers, it hadn't been the first time. Miss Camille must've known. Big sums going like that. But it wasn't Bea's place to say. She hadn't even talked about it in the kitchen; there was enough talk going on there as it was.

All day the chatter sang its way back and forth between Mrs Pikes and May. About people she didn't know and places she could never get straight in her head. The barmaid at the new road house just beyond Keswick. And the divorcee who'd taken The Priory at Portinscale for the summer. The lilting refrains and the pauses and the questions that were not questions at all that Bea could now follow almost as well as anyone. The pursed lips and the sucked-in breath and the arch glances that drew out always those curled smiles: Mrs Pikes to May and back again and May to Mrs Pikes.

Silent you thought it was when you stood outside with those empty hills closing round you and the still lake and the sky mirror-grey. But it was an endless murmur-

124

ing chain. A whispering that went round and round: one thing glimpsed and another overheard. Mrs Pikes's relatives and May's strung out among all the hill farms and half the kitchens of the big houses in Keswick. And all of them talking. About Miss Camille.

'Gets himself real dressed up for just old men and farmers' lads.'

May pulled another shirt from the pile in the wicker basket at her side and, sprinkling it with water, brought the heavy smoothing iron down on it in a cloud of steam.

Mr Brookes had taken to wearing white shirts open-necked with a silk cravat, often two in a day. Starched they had to be and blued, and ironed so not even the shadow of a crease showed. He'd got very particular all of a sudden. Snappish if something wasn't right. Unpredictable. Showing his underside, Bea said. Careless.

Mrs Pikes pushed her larding needle into the joint of beef in front of her with a sharp stab.

'P'raps he can't tell right from left when he gets to the main road at Grange?'

May sucked in her breath.

'You mean he doesn't go into Tommy Rigg's at all?'

'My cousin goes into Tommy Rigg's. Not often, mind, but he does and he says he hasn't seen him in there above half a dozen times.'

'Where does he get to then?' May darted a sly look at Bea, but Bea affected not to notice.

'There's all sorts of places. Turn right and there's that new hotel on the Seatoller road at Rosthwaite, that's just a couple of miles. Turn left and there's The Lodore.'

'My sister says there's people from London and all over come to stay at The Lodore. For the walking and that. It's that grand. They've got tea dancings and an American cocktail bar!'

'There you are! And there's Keswick itself not five mile away up the lake.' She threaded another strip of lard into her needle. 'He's been seen all over. Flash car like that doesn't pass unnoticed in these parts.'

*

You came up over the quiet hills and there it was, curving round the sheltered bay. Terrace after terrace of colour-washed houses going down to a blue sea.

'Never been to Brinksome?' they'd said. 'Oh, we'll have to show you Brinksome. Soon as the fine weather comes.'

They park the car on the esplanade in front of the painted stucco houses. Fairy lights are strung between lampposts all along the promenade and clusters of deck chairs stand in rows.

'What a picture!' says Moira getting out of the car, gazing up at the houses. But when she looks closer, their paint's peeling off and the twirling stems of the wrought-iron balconies are cracked with rust. And they aren't even houses at all. They're small hotels. Bed-and-break-fasts. They have squares of cardboard propped up in their front windows saying No Vacancies in sharp black letters. And some of the names over the doors have bits missing on their illuminated signs. A bulb gone, or a section of glass panel smashed and not replaced.

'Stroll along the prom, shall we?' suggests Nan.

'Girl on either arm. Come on,' insists Jeth, and winks at Moira.

There's quite a breeze. It slaps Moira's duster coat against her legs, twining it tight round her knees, making it difficult to walk. But when she plucks it loose the wind tears it out of her hand, flapping it wide open. And her hair, tugged free from its tight curls, blows across her face. All night she'd had it done up in hard metal curlers. All night, tossing and turning. Beside her Jeth strides on, like he's walking over the hill at Penbar-row after the sheep, squeezing her arm tight against his side. The coloured paving stones of the prom bounce up at her and the curving houses sway in and out of her sight, the swags of fairy lights dancing up and down as she stumbles along, and snatches of sea glittering and then gone as her hair whips back across her eyes. Jeth nearly has her off her feet. And every so often – squeeze

– would go his arm, tighter than ever. It takes her breath away. What if Nan saw? What if Nan knew? But she couldn't know anything, she's on the other side. Jeth's arm would be loose on that side, limp. Nan would never guess.

The deck chairs, when they get to them, are padlocked together in lines staring blindly out to sea. Another notice in sharp black lettering swings from a chain that ropes them off from the pavement.

'Fifteen pence!' exclaims Nan. 'Fifteen pence to sit down!'

'Fifteen pence!' they say to each other. And it keeps them going all the way along the front to the Pavilion. 'Fifteen pence! You can get a cup of tea for Fifteen pence!'

And they do. Biscuits eight pence extra.

'Don't have one of those shop biscuits,' whispers Nan, fishing in her carrier bag. 'I brought some date loaf.' She unwinds the clingfilm packet on her knee and they pass half-slices to each other under the table. 'We always do this,' she confides. 'Mind the butter on your coat.'

'Good bit of loaf, Nannie,' says Jeth. He can get a whole half piece into his mouth at once.

'Yes,' echoes Moira stiffly, in a voice stifled by crumbs. 'Very nice.'

The sea winks at them and dazzles their eyes. The crests of waves tip white and then are gone. No more than ripples, no more than a flash in the sun. And then gone. It's all you see, all you notice. While underneath, the weight of water pushes at the land and the land, unable to resist, is dragged back with it, down the rasping beach.

'You have to drive,' says Nan, 'to find the sheltered bays.'

'All the same sea, love.'

Moira stares out into the glittering blue. All the same sea, but at the cove near the Dingle the waves are sharper, icier, more insistent. Hungrier. Pull you out after them in a moment, far out; pull you down.

They go to Inchcombe and Warleigh and Porthrennock. Moira can't remember when she'd ever had such a time of it. Jeth making up to her, saying outrageous things. Looking at her so direct with those blue eyes. Right in front of Nan, too, sometimes. And Nan just laughing, telling him not to be such an old goat, and saying to Moira:

'Don't you take no notice of these farmers, they're all the same!'

But Moira knows. She can still see the blue eyes looking back at her from her bedroom mirror when she stands in the shadowy gloom of the empty house in the Dingle, when the banging of car doors and the goodbyes are over. And when she takes off her coat and pushes up the sleeve on her right arm she's sure she can still feel a faint bruise from all Jeth's squeezing. Impetuous, that's what he was. You wouldn't think it at first, you wouldn't think it to look at him. At Warleigh he'd wanted her to go down the pier with him. Put his arm round her shoulder, held it tight. She hadn't known where to put herself, Nan there, laughing. 'Come on!' he'd insisted in a loud whisper. She'd had to say no.

She wears all her best summer things. Something different she tries to have on every time. When she comes to the end of them she wants to buy more. Wants to have a new dress for every outing. But where can she buy anything with no shops for miles? Only shops she sees are in the towns Jeth and Nan take her to. When Jeth finally dozes off under his handkerchief and Nan says: 'Let's go and have a gander, you and I,' they stroll off down the High Street. Arm in arm. Like sisters.

'Look at this Moirey! Look at that!'

All sorts of shops, but she can't buy anything. Nan would see. Nan would guess.

She tries on dresses of Lou's, but they're all so old. Besides, they give her the creeps.

It's at Porthrennock that Moira produces the salmon spread sandwiches. They order the pot of tea and when the waitress has gone, and before Nan can rummage in her bag, Moira unclicks the gilt clasp of her handbag and draws them out.

'I brought something . . .' she murmurs, feeling her cheeks flush.

They beam at her, shifting on their chairs as she unfolds the plastic covering clumsily on her knees.

'Well, there's a treat.'

'. . . salmon spread,' she whispers.

'Salmon spread!'

At Windover they're having a fair. They can't get near the sea to park. A hurdy-gurdy, and photo-booths with funny cut-out faces, and winkles in little greaseproof paper bags, and ice cream. You can throw quoits and win china. Or shoot rifles and win – anything your heart desires. It's all there, on the stall, piled up in a vast pyramid. Laid out tier after tier up into the stained canvas ceiling.

Out on the front, a doll beats another doll to death with a white-painted stick and then kicks the lifeless heap of rag under the blue and white striped awning behind him.

'Oh dear,' he squawks in a sing-song voice. 'Oh deary me.' No sooner is the dead doll out of sight than another appears on the stage. In policeman's clothes. The first doll turns sharply at his approach. 'Judy?' he shrieks. 'Judy? Never seen her!'

On the beach they have tea that they buy in paper cups from a van with a grimy black smoke-stack and adverts for Pepsi and Lyons Maid all over its sides. Moira dozes off listening to the sound of the sea. But it isn't down at the edge of the sand where it should be, but somewhere under her head. Moving restlessly. Back and forth. Its echo caught in the ears of the tiny whorled shells that lie on the beach all around her. Up. And back. Up and . . . A huge, breathing, sighing sound. The sun beats down and in her sleep she licks vainly at the edges of her dry lips. Under the thin crust of sand it's all water, all sea. Fathomless. Rolling her with it over and over, up and back.

She wakes with a shadow falling across her face. Something sharp cutting into her forehead. She puts up her hand. Opens her eyes. Jeth is kneeling in the sand beside her, grinning, blotting out the sun. Her fingers touch a cardboard brim, a flat, cardboard crown.

'You were getting that red, Moira,' Nan's voice comes from somewhere behind Jeth, 'we thought you'd better have a hat.'

She struggles to sit up and her hand knocks it. It begins to slip sideways.

'Don't take it off,' murmurs Jeth. And leans forward. And kisses her. On the mouth.

'Oh Jeth!' shrieks Nan in a bubbling cascade of laughter. 'Don't muss her about!'

'Oh!' gasps Moira.

The hat rolls off into the sand and lies there.

'Kiss me quick! Kiss me quick!' it says all round its brim.

Now that it was summer it had taken to raining every day. Not real rain. But rain that just hung in the air like a wet curtain. So fine you had to look twice to see it. Miss Camille was always standing at the window, looking out. Looking to see if it had stopped. Or started again. You had to look close. One minute it would be there, next minute it was gone. Like Mr Brookes. And you could never tell how long he'd be gone for. Sometimes it would just be the half-hour and there he'd be striding in through the door with the newspaper or the packet of fags, or whatever the excuse had been that time. Other times two hours would go by. Three. And Four.

It got, Bea said, so that every time they heard the car go off, the silence that came in after seemed to fall on them heavier and heavier, pressing down on them like a weight. Like something in a bad dream. The floor caving in and all of them tumbling with it to another level of the house, somewhere murky and suffocating, shut in. They could have pushed their way out of it, they could have thrown open windows and doors; they could have spoken. But they were caught in something sticky that held them all silent.

They knew now, in the kitchen, where Mr Brookes went. At first he'd been seen all over. But lately he'd been seen always turning into the same driveway on the outskirts of Keswick, the car hidden straight away by the deliberate curve of laurels and rhododendron bushes. The lady's maid who opened the door to Mr Brookes was said to be French and wouldn't give the time of day to anyone. But the between-stairs maid, who rushed to press her nose to the bars of the basement window every time she heard the car draw up, was Mrs Pikes's own niece and had instructions to miss nothing.

'Flowers,' Mrs Pikes would report. 'A whole sheaf of hothouse lilies! And chocolates, the day before, in a great velvet box.'

There were no arch smiles now; no laughter. They kept their heads bent to the scraping of carrots or the mixing of dough and in their heads, Bea said, the guilty knowledge that it was all being paid for with Miss Camille's money. It was like a shame, Bea said, that they all felt. But what could they say if Miss Camille wouldn't say it first.

Miss Camille went on like nothing was different, nothing was wrong. Out of her morning dress and into her afternoon frock. Up for her evening bath and down for her drink. Sitting waiting for him in that dead room. All the empty, sagging chairs round her and the piles of old journals and children's games of people who hadn't been children for years. She wouldn't have a lamp lit, not even for company. She'd just sit there looking out towards the windows. The evening sun coming in low would make everything glow for a moment – the sherry in Miss Camille's glass and the glass itself winking and sparkling. Everything warm. Golden. Everything perfect for a moment. Perhaps she waited for that? Then the light going back inch by inch leaving shadows to grow in the corner of the room. And then, from hill to hill, would come the cavernous echo of farm dogs barking. There was no dog at Fernlea, only silence. And the thin pencil line of smoke going up from the cigarette burning in the ashtray next to Miss Camille's glass.

She'd started lighting cigarettes and leaving them to burn. She carried a packet with her all over the house, and a little jade lighter. She'd pick one up sometimes and hold it, burning, in her fingers and the smoke seemed to make her eyes water. But Bea never saw her smoke it, any more than she would hardly touch her drink. Except to hold it. To pick it up. And then put it down again. It was all – it was all – edgy. It was all indecision.

When he was there she'd match him drink for drink. Bea couldn't take her eyes off her. No more could he. Like a fox watching a goose. She'd sip at her cocktail all ladylike, scarcely wetting her lips and then, as if she couldn't bear the taste of it any more, she'd lift her head and tilt back the little glass. You could see her body shudder and her lower lip all wet from it and a dribble run quickly and silently down the side of the glass and seep in a coloured stain into the frilled paper mat.

'Ghastly!' she'd say. Something like that.

But he'd already be halfway over the room to her, his own glass in one hand, the cocktail shaker in the other.

'Fill you up, old girl, eh?' And he'd lean against her chair, his thigh pressed into her shoulder. 'Delicious,' he'd murmur, 'real winner, this one.' And the drink would splash into her glass, out quick as a lie from the silver mouth, colourless as air. Sometimes there was a froth of bubbles on it, sometimes it was thick as oil curling up the sides of her glass: green, or yellow. Blue. It made you shudder just to look at it. 'Delicious!' he'd say and the smile would curve up into his moustache.

But he didn't always get her where he wanted her. Sometimes the drink made her sharp. Hard-faced and hard-voiced and scarcely able to rein it in. One evening, as Bea was offering a dish of buttered parsnips to Miss Camille at table, he announced he was going to be out all the next day. Been invited shooting by a bloke he'd met in Tommy Rigg's, he said. The serving spoon stopped in mid-air.

'You don't shoot,' she said, the words gone hoarse in her throat.

'How d'you know?' He grinned at her, lolling back in his chair, twirling his wine glass round and round on the polished table. 'Just 'cause you've never seen me?'

'And what are you going to shoot? In *July*!'

He coloured up then, the blood rising so quickly in his cheeks and draining away again you might just have thought it was anger.

'Oh,' he waved the glass airily, like he couldn't care. 'Links says the place is teeming with rabbits and stuff. Get our eye in before the game season.'

'Links?' said May and Mrs Pike to each other. 'Links? There's no Links in the district and certainly not round Buttermere.'

First time he went he came back empty-handed. No gun, no catch – he could've been anywhere. He saw it on our faces. After that, whenever he was supposed to be off shooting, he always brought back something: a brace of pigeons or a rabbit. She pretended to take no notice. But they did in the kitchen.

'Well, our Bea, what's this?' said Mrs Pikes when Bea carried in the first brace of pigeons.

'Couple of ducks.' Bea dropped the pigeons onto the table and, screwing up her face in disgust, went to wash her hands at the sink.

'Where'd he get these?' sang out Mrs Pikes, lifting them up.

'Shooting.'

Mrs Pikes shook her head.

'He never shot these, not today; they're clay cold. And nobody round here'd tie their legs together with anything fancier than a snatch of baler twine. Look at this.' She tugged at the string. 'Butcher's twine!'

Towards the middle of August he came back with a grouse.

'Glorious twelfth!' he said, swinging it on its string, full of himself.

'Take it out, Bea,' said Miss Camille, looking up from her book.

They had it roast four days later.

'This my bird?' he demanded, almost bouncing in his chair.

Miss Camille looked across to where Bea was serving.

'This? I think this might have come from Roper's; their window had game in it when we drove through Keswick yesterday.'

You could have heard a pin drop. And then he laughed. Short little bark.

'Mine still hanging, is it? Going putrid?'

She rang early that night for Bea to run her bath. She'd started not sleeping and the chemist in Keswick had suggested a mustard bath before retiring. 'Banishes that "too tired to sleep" feeling,' it said on the tin. The chemist said he couldn't recommend it too highly, no end of ladies found it beneficial.

Miss Camille followed her up so soon, Bea'd only just got the taps turned on and the towels laid out. She didn't even hear the door close over the noise of the water thundering into the tub. Miss Camille just appeared in amongst the steam.

'Oh Miss!' exclaimed Bea, 'you did make me jump. I've done the powder an' that.'

But Miss Camille just stood there looking agitated and absent all at the same time, her brow knit and her breath coming heavy as if she'd run up the stairs. She pulled an envelope slowly out of her pocket, her hand over the face of it as if she was still hiding it. Bea saw the paper trembling.

'Bea,' she said, 'will you take this to Keswick for me tomorrow morning and post it? It's – it's to my brother; I want him to come up here.'

Bea held out her hand for the letter, but Miss Camille didn't seem able to relinquish it. 'Bea, if you are noticed on the road by – by anyone driving . . .' A flush burst up into her cheeks and her voice lowered itself to a fierce whisper. '. . . if your absence is commented on by anyone – well, it will be commented on by everyone – you had better say you have asked to change your day off this week. But Bea, make sure no-one sees this letter. Be sure you don't mention it to anyone. Even if you have to make up all sorts of fibs.'

*

Alone she must have thought herself. As alone as if she had been transported to a desert. As confined as if there were bars and leg irons. And wherever she turned, the grin of her jailer. No escape to the sea, to the long, thundering waves; no boat ever put into Belle Plage. And none to the marsh. Where could she go, knowing no ways through it? What help could she find in it? Only the reeds closing in round her. And the stumbling foot slithering into lying water, halting her, trapping her. The wind carrying away her cries and the quake sucking at her, pulling at her. Like he did. Like . . .

There was only the track. Only the labouring over the rough ground, the weaving from ridge to ridge, breath a gasp in her throat and sweat little glistening trails down her neck. At the bend in the track before Pont St Honore there was time to roll down her sleeves hiding the marks, the red weals and the deep sullen bruises. To slow her pace. To even out the dip and sway of her gait though the pain of it showed still in her face; drawing it, blanching it. There were women in Pont St Honore – women who fell silent at her approach. Women who watched her pass without expression on their faces. Jean-Luc's mother's sister among them. And the words died away on her lips. But they saw, all of them. Without need for words. They read it, in her face. And kept themselves silent. They could have told her the way things would go. They could have warned her. They remembered, many of them, the young boy with the sly look creeping over his face and deceit already showing in his eyes and the grubby hands inside which there was always some broken maimed thing. Some fly with torn-off wings or a beetle with half its legs crushed or its antennae torn out, blundering in crazed circles. And the look on his face when he showed you. He was always in trouble – things broken, thing stolen. And always the sly grin that grew ever more furtive. In showing off, in courting the admiration of the other children of Pont St Honore, he went so far he found himself in a no-man's land where the others would not follow. He lost himself. And from then on they kept their distance. The little boy was grown to a man, but still there was that same look in the eyes, the same grimy hands and quick-bitten nails.

Delving, pinching, paddling fingers they had become. Bold, with the quickly dawning knowledge that here was a person who could not turn from him. No doubt she and Jean-Luc had spoken only of skills that could be brought to the marriage. Of money put by. Of the number of rooms in the house. The promise of duties. That there was more implied hung over all their dealings. As she sewed her linen for the marriage bed no doubt she thought of it. As she lay those last few weeks in her sister's house no doubt she listened, through the quiet of the house, to the creakings or the silence from the next room. And thought it something contained and fleeting, like the mating of birds. Something to be endured and soon over. Something, perhaps, infrequent. No doubt she had not thought that desire could run like a stain, colouring not only the night, but the day too. That it could burn in the blood like a marsh ague, so that your belly hollowed and your arms ached from it and your hands could settle to nothing but the soft touch of flesh beneath them.

That August, the nights were close. With the long pools dried and the banks of the cuts showing lower, the smell of mud hung in the hot air. Dried mud and mud newly exposed: the decayed body of the marsh, so long buried, now raised and breathing in the thick night air.

They kept their windows open and their door, but the heat pressed as close indoors as out. The lamp that burned on their kitchen table lit up the bare room like the stage of a playhouse. Each night, to Leon's watching eye, the shadow of the broom handle leaned across the cavernous space beside the looming arc of the bucket. And the end of the twist of string that hung over the half-empty shelf on the wall dangled like a rope. Night bugs flung themselves against the glass chimney of the lamp and moths crawled on its globe. Jean-Luc and she sat in the centre of this stage, silent and bedraggled with the heat. He with his shirt collar flung open and she with wisps and strands of hair fallen from their pins and trailing wetly down over the back of her neck or hanging heavy over her sallow cheeks. Each on a hard-backed kitchen chair drawn close to the table. The hot, bare room with its scarcely wavering shadows like a cave around them and they two creatures who crouched, wary, at its centre.

Always she had some work to her hand over which she kept her head bent. She never looked at him, though there was the sense that she watched him constantly, her body keeping the watch for her so that her eyes might hold themselves turned away from him. But if she thought so to deflect his interest, then she had reckoned without him. For he glanced across at her often, shy covert glances. Some nights he might have his gun broken open before him, or be knotting up a trapping net where it had torn. Most often he swung idly on his broken-backed chair, tipping himself backwards and forwards, one foot pushing against the table leg.

One night Leon saw in his hand the flash of a knife. He twirled it, its point dug into the table top. He drew it down the cracks in the wooden surface, little runnels of dirt skittering before it. And he watched her close from beneath lowered eyelashes as he made the blade scrape against the wood with a harsh, shrieking sound. Up and down he went, up and down. And not a look exchanged or a word spoken. But cat and mouse it was. Back and back she drew herself, by hair's breadths. But he saw. And when she was forced to stretch her hand over the table for more thread for her mending, then he pounced. The knife point pinioned her arm to the table, her flesh mounding up white around the point.

'You'd best not pull away this time, ma belle,' he drawled.

But she could not help herself. A bright bead of blood sprang up from the knife.

'Tha's a sharp little thing, my skinning knife.'

'You're mad!' she whispered, the words hissing out at him. 'Let me go!'

'Not till you come over here. You ain't given me no kiss since suppertime.'

She made no move.

'You want this knife on your pretty lips instead, then?' He grinned and wriggled in his chair and from her arm a thin trickle of blood ran quickly over the white skin. 'Little cut for every kiss you won't give? You won't forget again in a hurry; salt wind keep 'em raw for days.'

Leon saw how stiff she sat on his knee. Saw, clear, the disgust that twisted her face as she turned away her head from the darting bite of his kisses. How she held herself taut against the head bobbing at her neck and his hands that pulled at the stuff of her blouse. Her knuckles clenched in her lap; her fingers fluttered as if to push him away and then fell back again.

Another night, the heat drove her out of her chair to stand against the frame of the open window. So close Leon could have reached out and touched her. She pushed her damp hair back from her forehead and, drawing her hand down her cheek, laid it against her neck. Her fingers as though of their own accord slowly began to undo the top button of her dress. Like the stoat on the rabbit, without a sound Jean-Luc was on her. Leon saw how his pleasure leaped hearing her gasp, feeling her jerk against his hands. He caught her arms tight and held her to him.

'Too hot, eh, ma belle? Too hot?'

And bending over her shoulder began to lick at the little trails of sweat on her neck.

She writhed and sobbed and her fingers clawed at the air. But his tongue only worked at her the harder, his head bending lower and lower, his fingers pulling at the buttons on the front of her dress. At last she wrenched herself free and hobbled away beyond Leon's sight. Jean-Luc, slack-mouthed and grinning, let her go. Leon saw only the quick, hooking movement of his left leg and heard the crash as Laurette fell and then the sharp cries that subsided in a strangled, gargled sound and the muffled noise of scraping against floorboards that fell into silence.

In the kitchen of our cottage Leon held himself still at this point in his tale and then clapping his hands to his ears and letting his head fall with a crash against the wall beside him, he banged out on the floor the unmistakeable rhythm. On and on it went as if he could not stop himself – as if he had not been able to tear himself away. At last the violence of it subsided but still he hung there, his face to the wall, his hands clenched over his ears, shaking his head from side to side.

*

That Thursday at the Old Folks Club, pouring tea from the heavy enamel teapot into rows of cups, Nan says to Moira and Elsie Layce helping with the milks and sugars: 'Had a nice little treat on Tuesday, took ourselves off to Lynne. We had a lovely crab supper.'

Moira doesn't answer. Can't answer. Can't speak for the rage that boils up inside her. Hotter than the water bubbling in the urn. Went off to Lynne? Without her! She picks up a tray of full cups and marches off down the line of chairs. Sulks all afternoon. Doesn't care who sees her. Doesn't care what they say. Doesn't think what she's done till she gets back to the house in the Dingle. Till the coolness and the silence and the smallness of the house close in around her. Always been so careful. Never put a foot wrong. Moira, Moira!

'Getting above herself.'

'Spoiled.'

'Taking advantage.'

'Always tears afore bedtime.'

'Shouldn't go poaching another woman's husband.'

'Was she?'

'Well . . .'

'You never see that old car of Jeth's now but there's three of them in it.'

'Three's company.'

'Two's company.'

'Which one of 'em's the odd man out?'

They keep their voices low in the parlour of The Ram's Head. Dropping into silence when Davy bangs open the door, sliding quickly into murmuring discussions of live-stock yields and cricket scores. Davy grown a look on him black as a badger. Won't talk to no-one. Sits by the hearth-stone, dog at his feet, staring at a newspaper spread out on the table. Never turning a page.

At the end of two weeks Nan goes down to the Dingle. Down by the path through Leeve's Wood, so no-one would see her. Carrying roses wrapped in wet newspaper. Moira opens the door to her. Stands on the doorstep. Eyes gone small.

'These are for you. Got to have roses in June.'

'July tomorrow,' says Moira.

'Well, then,' says Nan following her down the narrow plasterboard hall to the kitchen, 'just in time.'

Moira pulls back the wet paper. Nan's pink roses, still warm from the wall of the farmhouse. The musky scent fills the kitchen.

'Stay for tea?'

'Just a quick one.'

As she fills the kettle, Moira watches Nan in the piece of broken mirror she keeps propped on the kitchen

141

windowsill. She sees how she leans first against the kitchen cupboard, then against the table. How she rests her fingertips on the table-top and draws them back quickly; touches the edge of the draining board and pulls them away.

Just like the doctor! thinks Moira. And turns off the tap so sharply the water-pipe judders all down its length.

'Not like your kitchen, is it?'

'Oh, mine – I get worn out walking round it. This is just right.'

They go down to the cove after tea. The sun in the late afternoon like pools of gold between the trees. The dappled shadow running before them, flickering brown and purple across the path. Nan stumbles once or twice. Moira, a step behind her, takes her elbow.

'You got to watch your step in the Dingle, Nannie,' she murmurs, too low for Nan to hear.

The waves lap at the shore, a curious milky white in the hazy sunlight. Moira lets go of Nan's elbow. Her thin mouth drops in a sullen curve.

'What's it so still for? Why's it so calm today?'

But Nan stares dreamily out at it. 'Don't know why we go driving all over the place,' she murmurs. 'So nice here. So peaceful.'

*

As the last blood-red swathes of the winter afternoon flared along the horizon and slowly drained from the sky, the Duke's sister, the Marchesa d'Sforo, arrived at La Pianta. In the glimmering of dusk, shadows thickened and the frost tightened its pincer-hold upon the land. Silence and cold and darkness descended once more. And then were suddenly broken by the leaping up of lights, the echo of shouting, the noise of running feet, hob-nails clattering against stone. Breath lifted in clouds above the lines of hastily assembled servants, and the smoky tang of frost and lighted torches swept in with a gust of cold air as the doors of La Pianta were flung open.

Accompanied by the yapping of her little Chinese dog cushioned against the bosom of her maid, the Marchesa sailed on a tippet-edged raft of brocade across the chequered floor of the hall. From beneath bowed heads, with covert smiles the household servants watched her accept the stiff embrace of her brother and incline her puffy cheek towards her sister-in-law. They knew why she came.

She lost no time. Installing herself before the fire in her parlour, her gouty foot on a footstool, her lap dog wheezing on a cushion beside the fender, she sent for her sister-in-law.

'You are well?' she demanded. The small eyes travelled slowly across the Duchess's body, up and down over the soft folds of silk, from breast to stomach and back again. 'You are . . ?'

Behind her, laying a gauze shawl over the doughy expanse of her mistress's shoulders, the Marchesa's maid stared at the Duchess with the same boldly inquisitive eyes.

'I am well, madam,' the Duchess replied icily.

One by one up the back stairs, and unnoticed from the recesses of dusty corridors, there crept those servants of the Duke who served also his sister. They came with stealth, looking about them cautiously before they approached the Marchesa's door, tapping on it so softly they would not have been heard if Barbara, her maid, had not been waiting for them just the other side of it. They slipped past her and, with practised silence, with no more than a sigh of displaced air, she drew it shut again. One by one they gave their intelligence, eyeing the ducat on the low table between themselves and the Marchesa, and crept out again leaving the Marchesa still unsatisfied despite their reassurance.

Tomaso knew them all. He knew without having

questioned them what each had to tell. As arranged, when dinner was over and the Marchesa sat alone before her fire, Tomaso came to her.

'How is your son, madam?' he asked as the maid removed her mistress's wig and began to brush out the thin curls pinned round her wrinkled forehead.

'My son? My poor boy! How *can* he be – with that creature installed?' she jerked her head towards the Duchess's apartments. 'All his hopes, his prospects! Now sole heir; now displaced; then sole heir again; and then displaced again. We cannot hope for such good fortune as we had with the first girl. This one is young and strong – I am assured she is not with child, but she will bear.'

'For "young" say rather "foolish" and for "strong" "wilful" and there, with God's grace, is your fortune again, madam.'

'What do you mean?'

Without her wig the family resemblance became startlingly close. The Marchesa bent towards him, narrowing her eyes and the firelight gleamed on the receding forehead and the balding temples so that her face appeared almost snout-like with little black darting eyes. It could have been Federico. In a dress.

Tomaso leaned from his chair to draw closer to her.

'Listen,' he said, 'and I will tell you.'

The Duke's sister did not continue her journey to Venice the next day, as was expected, or even the day after that. She stayed four days and nearly all of them were spent in the Duchess's parlour.

The Marchesa seemed to have cultivated a passion for music since she was last at La Pianta and nothing would satisfy her but that her sister-in-law play for her. The wild, mournful lays of the Duchess's homeland she pronounced charming but professed a longing for new songs. Did the Duchess not know any? None at all? The Marchesa became, it was said, quite animated.

'There was one – how did it go? – something like . . .' and here, much to the amusement of the assembled company, she began to beat time with a bejewelled finger and sing first this refrain and then that in a little cracked voice. Even the Duchess smiled. Then from the back of the room there was a light cry, a sharp, pouncing cry, and those who turned their heads quickly saw Barbara pull a sheaf of music from under a pile of papers. Filippo's music – just as Tomaso had told her. In the sudden hush, in the sudden buzzing airlessness of the room she was as bold as a cock crowing.

'Here's music, madam!'

No-one had thought to watch her. In the general diversion no-one had noticed how she moved around the room ferreting beneath this and that with subtle fingers. The Marchesa was quick to cover the icy silence.

'Ah!' She beamed around her as though it was delight she saw in the circle of darkened, anxious eyes. 'Bring it here, Barbara.'

Only the rain could be heard whispering against the window and the tortured hiss of the sap in the green logs on the fire as the maid wove her way between table and birdcage and settle and chair, a dancing, triumphant step, with a smile on her face and the music held out in front of her.

'Now then,' purred the Marchesa.

She peered closely at the music, turning back page after page clumsily with her plump, blunt, heavily ringed fingers. She looked up from the last one.

'Charming, my dear, charming – and all duets!'

There was nothing for it but that she would have one of her brother's pages called in. The Duchess protested: she had no wish to play further, she would not play further. But the Marchesa brushed her aside as if she had no more significance than one of those small, persistent summer flies.

'That boy Federico speaks so highly of, Barbara, the tall one, the pale one – send for him. Lorenzo..? Marco..?'

'Filippo, madam?'

She sat them close together. Elbow to elbow. Chair leg against chair leg. There was no help for it, there was only one copy of the music. But we could see how they held themselves stiffly apart, the one in fear, the other in anger – and neither able to refuse. We could see how Filippo's fingers trembled as they lay across the lute's mouth and how the blood had drained from the Duchess's cheek and the fire blazed up in her eyes. But stiff as they held themselves, in the playing they could not help but lean, now the one, now the other, towards each other, bending to see the music better. It could not be avoided that an elbow might touch an arm, a head might incline at the same moment as the other's head. In the end, despite themselves, the music caught them up. Against the far wall the Duchess's women shifted uneasily, as tense and anxious as bewildered cattle.

When they had finished, the Marchesa made them play again and then again. And still she would not let them go, but now it must be games. It was a clever progression. From riddles to forfeits to blind man's buff. From the exchange of words to the touching of hands and then to the blind clasping at bodies.

By the next day when the Marchesa summoned Filippo again the whole house knew of it. Most were of the opinion that it was to the good. Anything to bring a smile to the Duchess's face, they said. But others shook their heads solemnly and warned of the dangers of too much preferment. Favour from the wrong quarter could put a noose round a man's neck, they said. And others still were silent, silent then at least, the tickling of unease which they had felt at first now grown into something coiled that stirred and writhed and quieted itself again and lay so heavy that they could not bring themselves to speak of it. There was the footman, staring out over the crowded hall, whose attention was suddenly caught by the particular way that Tomaso bent over the Marchesa's hand as she paused to greet him one evening before dinner. He was as startled, as alarmed for no clear reason, as the girl who surprised Tomaso and the Marchesa's maid talking in low quick voices in a dusty recess of a little-used corridor on the top floor of the house. She felt her breath catch in her throat and her limbs seize up and, in her haste to pass them, she stumbled. For no comprehensible reason. And there were others. There was the server at the Duke's table. There was the youngest page who had slept next to Filippo in the dormitory and could not forget his haggard eyes and the low, sleep-torn whispering whose broken phrases he could scarcely catch and which now haunted his own dreams. All of them. And each of them – silent.

'And Filippo? Who was it called for Filippo?'

The Duke did not look up from the papers he was signing, but Tomaso saw the arm in its wide velvet sleeve stiffen, the thumb and forefinger tighten round the quill pen. The nib dug for a second into the thick parchment. He watched the fine spray of ink with a pleasure that, for once, crept out over his face. He sat at the side of one of the most powerful men in the state of Venice, but it was *his* power that was recorded indelibly onto that paper. He recollected himself quickly, automatically picking up the silver sander.

'It was – and that last page there, too, Your Grace, your signature just there – it was, I believe, just chance. The Marchesa would have music and Filippo was the first one found . . .'

Federico pushed the papers away with a dismissive hand.

'My sister is tone deaf.' His voice was derisive. The pale amber eyes, that turned to stare at Tomaso, blank, the irises closed, almost vanished in the thin winter light from the narrow window opposite Federico's table.

Tomaso could not hold that inhuman stare, few men

could. He turned to shake sand on the drying ink of the Duke's signature and the fear seemed to douse itself.

'The playing of your lady would restore hearing even to the deaf, Your Grace.' He paused and took a quick breath, keeping his face averted from Federico. 'The Duchess was first taught, perhaps by her mother, who herself played like an . . .'

'Get those letters despatched, Master Secretary . . .' Federico rose so quickly his chair was almost overturned, '. . . and send my sister to me.'

Alone again, Tomaso's face fell into soft, sulky lines, the bottom lip turned down at its corners, his eyelids lowered to hood his eyes. A clerk who had come from the main Secretariat, hearing the Duke depart, retired again stealthily without daring to knock. We two, trapped on either side of the single desk in the scribes' cubbyhole leading out of the Duke's study, working on an urgent lease for the Duke, we did not dare put pen to paper lest the scratching of our nibs reveal us. We had already seen, already heard, more than was safe for us to know. But Tomaso seemed to have forgotten us, or else he did not care. He kicked the outer door to and, having folded the letters, pulled towards him sealing wax, taper and tinder box. He lit the candle and twirled the stubby length of wax in its flame. A thin trail of black smoke twisted up from it into the shadows of the low embossed and raftered ceiling. He scowled at it and moved the wax stick further from the flame.

'So,' he whispered to himself, but we heard it, that hiss like a snake. 'So, my lord, so . . . you cannot bear even to hear the name of the Duchess's mother mentioned, so close is she still in your thoughts – so wound around your heart. There's many an enemy would like to have the ends of that tale in his hands to have the strangling of you with it! The passion of your loves – your first love I'll wager and hers – so overwhelming no passion has entered your heart since. The murder of her husband-to-be before his wedding day and no assassin ever found – that has your mark on it, the first of a long line. And heaven's revenge – the girl given instead to Count Treviso and dead within the year in childbed. But a fair daughter. Oh, so fair a daughter . . .'

Tomaso held the soft end of the wax down over the letters one by one and long slow drops of red fell onto the white paper where the folded ends of the sheet met.

'Blush for blush, mole for mole, glance for glance, a perfect copy of her mother? Save that *she* is not willing!' The voice drew itself out into a low chuckle and then the mouth pursed itself as if in mock pain and the head wagged slowly from side to side with relish. 'Not submissive, either; not meek before your will. What a cruel trick! The embraces of the dead are cold, are they not? But not as cold as the enforced embrace. You had not bargained on that, had you? No . . . And worse, now you suspect her of being stolen from you – it was not hard to bring you to that – stolen even before you possessed her. Lost before she was won! And by a page sent to woo her – as you were sent all those years ago, a page, to woo her mother for another. Ah, what a slow poison! But if you cast her from you there is no other likeness of her mother living – and all is lost.'

The voice faded into whispered breathing though the lips still moved, till there was only the sound of the letters turned end to end to end repeatedly in Tomaso's dextrous fingers so that their sharply creased sides tapped sharply against the table-top with the dead, forced sound of the joints of mechanical dolls made to dance by the pulling of levers.

Something lost. Something changed. The soft grass and the low trees bordering the stream and the dimpling of sunshine through the Dingle all there. But a pleasure lost. A brilliance in the world dimmed. And how to find it again? What to do to get it back?

Up through the wood, all the trees eerie and still as watchers to Moira's darting eyes. Up to the shop. Up to the knitting bee in the church room at the vicarage. The smile twisting on Moira's face with the effort of it. Up to the village hall to help with the old folks' teas. Fingers never able to keep still; pulling at her hair, fiddling with her beads, tugging her skirt straight, lining up the cups on the tray, over and over. Made you tired to look at her. And then she'd see she was doing it. She'd clasp one hand in the other, tight, so her knuckles showed, and walk away a few steps from where she'd been. But it wasn't long before one of her hands would slide away from the other and be reaching up to primp at a curl, or brush a speck from her cardigan. Soon as Nan appeared the fingers would fly even faster. You couldn't help but notice, couldn't help but see. And then, minute she spoke to her, soon as she smiled at her, they'd lie quiet. Still.

She put her through it, Nan. Stories of drives to the moor and trips to the sea, just her and Jeth. Almost skittish she was. Teasing. Like she knew what was going on in Moira's mind. But nothing broke that glassy calm, just nods and smiles echoing whatever Nan said.

They watch, in the post office and the shop and the

village hall, they watch her close. Watching for a display of temper like she'd had before. Behind her back they wink and smile.

'Working hard,' they say.

'Playing a waiting game.'

Pining away down in the Dingle. Pacing through the cardboard rooms of the little house, up and down the patched lino in the hall, back and forth to the front-room window twenty times a day. Three weeks since she's seen Jeth closer than the churchyard on a Sunday surrounded by half the village. At first she thought he'd come to her. She pictures it over and over, especially towards dusk. His tall diffident figure appearing always from between the same few slender trees, gliding over the marshy grass in front of her gate. He could slip away from evening milking, down through the wood; never be missed. Sometimes she sees herself run out to meet him, hears her feet, even, on the cinder path. Oh Jeth! she would whisper under her breath and feel his arms go round her, smell the cloth of his coat and hear him murmur in her ear as he brushed a stray tendril of hair from her cheek. So clear, so real it had to be true.

Then she thought he might write. Small blue envelope it would be with a small blue sheet of paper inside it, ruled feint with looping handwriting. 'My darling Moira . . .' She starts waking every day long before the post, into the fierce singing of birds and the grey light of dawn. But no letters come. Only a postcard from Ruby Forman and her husband in Malaga and a bill from the electric.

Three weeks she waits. And then she gets it into her head he's waiting for her. And she can't get it out again. Sees him so clear it drives her to desperation. Course he wouldn't make a move, he wasn't the type. He was waiting for her to come to him. Mooching about in the shadows, sitting on a hay bale in the darkest corner of one of the barns, his task – whatever it had been – finished long ago, winding baler twine endlessly between his fingers. She can smell the dusty closeness of straw. See the dark where no-one would see them. Convinced, she is. All precaution driven out of her mind.

She dresses herself up in her best navy shoes and pins on the china brooch of a basket of flowers and pushes her way, breathless, up through Leeve's Wood late one afternoon. But, hovering among the last bushes, she sees the farmyard's empty. Silent. She doesn't dare set foot in it. She can tell there's no Jeth in the barns, without even looking. And then, over by the tractor, something moves. Someone steps forward. At first she thinks it's Jeth. She feels herself stumble from the trees and hears a gasping cry in her throat. Only it isn't Jeth, it's Davy. With a rifle in his hands. She sees him look straight at her. And raise it. She hears the shots burst out one after the other and the rooks rise up over her head in a screaming cloud and the clatter of waxy rhododendron leaves slapping into her as she turns and runs. And something fall onto the ground behind her with a muffled thud. She hears it for days after.

She can hardly bring herself to leave the Dingle after that. Can't bear to show her face in the village. The afternoon of the next knitting bee she gets a sick headache, thinks she can't face it.

'Oh Jeth!' she sobs into the bathroom mirror.

But if she wants Jeth she has to go.

She's so late by the time she sidles in, she's the last one there.

'Well now, Miss Thompson, and we almost thought you weren't coming.'

'Afternoon Mrs Wickham, Mrs Matt,' she takes a deep breath, 'Nan.' Blood racing and heart pounding and the heat suddenly prickling all along her skin, hot under her macintosh. She puts down her handbag, swaying a little against the big, central table. 'It's that pull up through Leeve's Wood. I'm getting slower and slower.' She gives a little fluttering giggle. 'At least I wasn't carrying any heavy shopping!' Hands trembling so much they won't keep still, better keep them busy, better keep them moving; fussing over the handle of her handbag, passing over the skeins of wool lying on the table. 'Mrs Wickham, I'd better have some more wool for blanket squares; just whatever you've got. Couple of skeins.' She turns back to Nan. 'Would you have a moment to wind on a few balls? I'm starting some new this afternoon.'

They sit side by side. Nan holds the skein on her plump arms and Moira winds the ball of wool from it, her quickly moving hands going back and forth. Back and forth. Chasing the strand of wool. Around them the clatter of needles and the chatter of tongues rising and falling. But Nan and Moira are silent. Right to the end of the winding, as if they're winding the silence itself, measuring it. Until the last few inches, then: 'Talking of shopping,' Nan says, 'we're going into Tremorne Thursday to stock up, if you want to take the opportunity to get some heavy stuff? We'll have the car.'

So the outings begin again. But Moira feels only an increasing sense of disappointment; an anxiety. She insists on taking them out to tea when the shopping's done, but it's not like before. They don't have any cling-film packets to unwrap on their knees. And eating bought biscuits makes them all feel formal, fall silent. It's not a treat at all. And Jeth doesn't even try to touch her. Doesn't take her elbow or put his arm round her shoulders. Not once. Not even at the end, when he backs the car up the uneven lane of the Dingle where it peters out and the path begins and they get her bags out of the boot – the flour and the sugar and the potatoes and all. And Jeth says: 'I'll carry these for you, Moira,' with something like his old smile.

She unlocks her front door with hands that shake so much she's sure he's seen. And goes ahead of him down the passage, just like she'd pictured it all those times. The kitchen, when she reaches it, seems to be buzzing

153

with a strange, high noise, so she can't hear Jeth ask where to put the bags, and dizzying electric lines dance in the air like a heat haze so she can't see straight. She hangs there, all the world gone far away, heavy against the door, waiting for his arms to go round her. She can't move, she can't speak. Nor can Jeth, it seems. Before she knows where she is, he's backing out of the room, vanishing in a blur up the hallway. She has to screw up her eyes to see him. And then the front door closes itself, a sharp, quiet sound in the empty house. And there she is, all alone again, with the warm smell of him still in the house and the blur clearing and the buzzing noise fading. To nothing.

It was Nan made him shy, kept him away. And Davy. She knows it. Davy's never liked her.

The stream's down to nothing when she crosses it the following Tuesday, the wood limp and sullen, the bright green long faded to dullness. And the main street of Sladdacoombe all dust and the flowers gone over. They're talking about the Churchwomen's outing when she pushes open the door of the parish room. They take the sulky look on her face for tiredness after the hot walk.

Nan's gayer, more sparkling than ever. 'You coming, Moira?' she calls. 'On the outing?'

Moira has to force the smile on her face. They don't notice, all of them taken up with the laughing.

'To Tintagel!' says Mrs Wickham, all aglow.

Moira drops into the empty chair next to Nan.

'Coach ride, two-course lunch, two hours' free time and return, all for five pound!' Nan's eyes dancing. She leans back in her chair looking round at the others. 'Day away from the men, eh!' She had everything, Nan. Just like Lou. 'You coming, Moirey? If we put our names down in pairs we can sit together on the coach.'

Moira sees it then. Clearly. She looks up at Nan, no smile or anything, just a straight look.

'Yes,' she says slowly, drawing it out. They all think

in the room it's strange, as if she's coming out of a dream. 'Yes,' she says and smiles, so that straightaway the strangeness gets forgotten, 'yes, we'll go together.'

*

In the heat, in the waiting silence of those afternoons when even for a time the wind lay still, you could almost hear the reed above your head split along its length: a long thin rippling sound. All over the marsh. The flowering of the reed it was. August gone and September come and still the slow splitting of the reed spears, the soft wet hairs of the tassle dark and curled into themselves clinging to either side. They lift. They rise proud from the leaves. And the wind parts them.

In among the reeds she walked, with her town eyes not seeing them, not seeing their flowering. In among that dancing up and down a heavy, slow thing. Up the track, up to Pont St Honore. Up to Madame Bouride's. A letter hid, like as not, under the cloth in her basket, tucked into the pocket of her dress. You could always tell where it was. As you approached her, her hand would move, quick as a fish in a stream, to where it lay, covering it protectively. And across her eyes a quick drawing-in, as if she had come now to suspect every man. She did her best to hide it with a smile and a word. But you could see it there still, behind the smile, behind the brave word. 'Bonjour' the only word there was left to her to exchange with anyone. All that she might say, all that no doubt she longed to tell, flattened and compressed – buried – in that one word. And all else silence, stretching out around her. Our silence. And hers. And yet the thing going on; far from sight, far from sound of anyone, for all the world as if in silence.

It was no wonder that the letters should increase, for at the last they were all she had. But whether answer ever came back from her sister at Amiens, we never knew. No strangers came to Pont St Honore that

155

autumn, no woman, nor no man – the brother-in-law that she insisted had been so particular on her account. Only the black geese. And then, as the days waned, the goldeneye.

The marsh became dense with fowl. Birds gathering to leave and others arriving. And with the first storms clouds of common birds driven from the sea and the shore: gull and tern and dunlin. Jean-Luc, who during the summer had gone mainly after sport with his ferrets, now took up his gun again. Not with the restraint, the knowledge of the fowler, but with a wildness that was a danger to man and bird. He did not creep out at dawn to position himself in the marshes, beat up the sleeping birds and shoot them as they flew. He had no need, they came to him. He had no more to do than sit on his front steps and watch as the drifts and skeins of fowl circled lower and lower over his head, settling to their old haunts on the long pools before him, pick up his gun and fire into their midst. We heard him over and over throughout those days, the flustered cries of the birds and the rapid shots. It was not a shoot, it was a massacre. Day after day. He drove the fowl from the Etaing de Marais and Le Beurre and pursued them out over the marsh. He shot at anything for the pleasure of seeing it fall to him. He shot more than he could sell to the dealer who sent his cart bumping down the track twice a week. Where the bodies floated out of his reach he left them. The red ochre that oozed up out of the marsh around these pools snaked out over the water to meet the twisting skeins of blood floating in from the corpses and the bodies drifted back and forth low in the water and came to rest bobbing against the reeds, where they rotted. Half of them inedible to begin with, or rarities that no other man would shoot on account of their beauty. Maybe he did not see that beauty. More like the sight of it maddened him to spoil it.

There came in to his eye now a watching look behind its slyness, a black thing ready to dart out at the least provocation. We saw how the swagger of his step took on a kind of drunken sway. How he dropped things and then kicked them aside. How he lashed out at his dog and frequently missed his mark. Up in Madame Bouride's he straddled his chair and boasted of his skills. And got only silence back from the men who sat around him.

*

No sooner had we watched the Marchesa's carriage disappear behind the curving hedges of the driveway of La Pianta and reappear, flickering to our sight, between the double line of cypresses. No sooner had the echo of horses' hooves and the jangle of harness died away along the road and the winter countryside drawn itself in again, grey and silent. Or the buzz of speculation over the Marchesa's tight-lipped departure subsided – for brother and sister always parted thus for one matter of displeasure or another. Than Tomaso called us together and announced that within the week the Duke himself would remove to Venice. Tomaso spoke out of a folded face. Like a piece of linen washed of all marks; all lines gone, ironed away and the thing folded meticulous and neat. A blank face. Wiped of all striving, all calculation. It was not just the power he had over us – it was he who drew up the list of those who would accompany the Duke. It was more than that. Tomaso had come to some – achievement. We dared not look at each other, we two who had overheard him in the secretariat when he had thought himself alone. But we were lost among the general whispering. The whispering that rose and fell and trailed off down every corridor as we made our way back through the house to our work.

The first whisper was of who would go and who would stay. And the second that followed close after was – why so soon? Every year at the Feast of Christmas the Duke went to the family house in Venice. But, unlike his sister, who made sure she installed herself sufficiently early so that not one ball, one levee, one fashionable gathering at Mass or the card-table might be missed, the Duke prevaricated always, delaying his departure. He would not go for Christmas, his household said bitterly, but he would stay for Lent! They fretted every year as he delayed, that icy fogs would descend on La Pianta, or the wind turn and sweep down from the Alps bringing blizzards, preventing them from setting out at all. And all the while Venice shimmered there beyond them, leaping with colour and light. Music floating on the sharp night air and quick footsteps on cobblestones beneath windows and the creaking passage of gondolas black against the glittering water. While they kicked their heels at La Pianta.

'It must be for the Duchess's sake that he removes so early,' went the talk. And there was little other reason to be seen; by the look on his face he took no joy in it. All eyes were turned to her, but no pleasure could be found there either. It was said by some that she had asked leave to visit her father, but that the Duke had denied her.

'He'll have no smiles now!' they said. 'There'll be no merry-making there. No Christmas games.'

But others shook their heads and laid their fingers along their noses.

'She will not lack,' they said, 'in Venice. She will be well-provided for. She will not keep her – unbending – long.'

They thought of the warmth of great fires and the close hiss of silk skirts and hands meeting and parting; the scent of perfumes and spice and whispering behind masks and brilliantly lit rooms, tier upon tier of flickering candles and long tables with feasts laid out in one marble palace after another, where the dark water lapped up to the white steps, the marble glimmering up at the moon from beneath black ripples. They talked of nothing else. Anyone who had seen Venice became an authority, the centre of a knot of eager listeners.

The morning that the names were given out of those who would travel with the Duke's household to Venice, Tomaso stalked from group to group pointing with his long index finger from one man to another.

'You and you – and you.'

He knew where to find each man. From the Duke's bedchamber to the stableyard. The talk died as his approach was caught sight of and did not start up again till long after the whisper of his footfall had vanished into silence.

He came first to us in the secretariat. We saw him leave the Duke's study, we saw him close the door with obsequious care. And as he turned we caught the flash of a sneer curl from the ends of his mouth which, by the time he had turned fully, had vanished.

'You and you and you will go tomorrow. You and you,' he said, pointing at us as though he was singling us out with purpose, as though he knew we had overheard him, 'will travel two days later with the Duke himself.'

We fell silent, looking from one to the other. Those who were going and those who were not. When, all of a sudden, Filippo burst from the Duke's ante-chamber and ran along the corridor after Tomaso. We heard only the pounding of his feet and his call: 'Signor! Signor!' His voice was faint to us, but not to others closer by.

'He did not care,' they said, 'who heard him. His eyes like dark holes in his head and his face the colour of ashes. He grabbed Tomaso by the sleeve, just on the turn to the Duchess's landing. "Signor!" he cried. But Tomaso shook him off. "You will not venture here if you value your life," he snarled at him. Filippo seemed not to have heard him, he clutched at Tomaso's arm again. "I cannot go to Venice, I cannot. Choose someone else, signor, I cannot go." His words fell over each other running on and on, running higher and higher the more Tomaso tried to silence him. Tomaso pushed him back against the wall, pinioning him, but Filippo's head still shook itself from side to side. "I cannot travel," he mumbled,

"I cannot travel." He squinted up at Tomaso. "I am sick."
"Dead or alive," Tomaso hissed between clenched teeth,
"you will be carried on that boat. Now, get back to your
post." He dropped his hands from Filippo's shoulders and
turned away. And Filippo slid to the floor.'

The story flew around the house. But even the wonder
that Filippo should not want to go to Venice was eclipsed
by the story that ran after it.

Tomaso had gone next to the apartments of the Duchess. She was having her hair dried after a bath, the long
wet ropes of it spread out on towels over her shoulders
and three of her women standing around her with more
towels patting and squeezing it dry strand by strand.
But Tomaso would not be denied admittance. He pushed
aside the woman who barred his way. He bowed low as
he entered her withdrawing room.

'Madam,' he said, but his voice was as curt as if he
spoke to a stranger, 'the Duke would have you make
yourself ready to leave for Venice in three days' time.
You may take two of your women with you, but since I
must know who they are, kindly point out to me which
they will be.'

The Duchess did not move. She sat as if enthroned on
her chair, the wet towels like some mantle round her
shoulders, staring straight ahead of her as though
Tomaso did not exist. She would not speak. She would
not look at him. Her knuckles were white where she
gripped the arms of her chair as though she was no
longer flesh and blood but bone only, and the silence in
the room a tangible, buzzing thing that preyed on everyone present. She would not answer him and so he
answered for her.

'Very well, madam,' he said. 'Very well.' And out came
the officious finger. 'You shall take her and her.'

Now! went the leaping whispers, now Tomaso has over-
reached himself! And they stood back, as it were, just
a low murmur between them all, bound by the same
expectation, waiting for an outburst from the Duke. Or

the Duchess. But there was none. The day went on and the Duke kept to his rooms. Not in withdrawal, but in a burst of new energy that kept us at our desks, while the boxes of documents accumulated on Tomaso's table. Food was carried up to him. And the trays taken down later, empty. The undercurrent of anticipation dwindled like candles guttering one after the other. And in the way that darkness creeps in after the last candle is extinguished, so silence began to creep along the passageways of La Pianta, a hollow, cold silence tense with new understanding.

By mid-afternoon there were only rays and gleams of thin winter sunshine wandering the landings and staircases of the great house. And into these, as lost and tentative as the stray shafts of light, came the Duchess. Dressed formally, for receiving in the afternoon, though none there were to be received by her and all who saw her in her progression along the landings and up and down the picture gallery, passing and re-passing the Duke's apartments, hid from her. She descended finally to one of the smaller sitting rooms and an unwilling footman was hastily despatched to light the fire for her. There she sat, as she had never sat before, making conversation with her ladies, the two ladies who were to accompany her to Venice, talk that fluttered and died in the growing shadows.

None of the household went near her, not the Duke nor Tomaso. She announced, after waiting, no doubt, for them, her intention to dine. She dined alone. Course after course was brought to her and, tiptoeing at the shoulders of the footmen who served her, came servants from the kitchens and beyond to stare, from the safety of the darkness behind the door, at her in her lonely circle of light, and cross themselves.

The next day, out she came again, walking the empty corridors, her eyes raised to whomever she encountered, a half-smile sometimes trembling on her lips. Below stairs they shook their heads.

'It is too late,' they murmured to each other, keeping their eyes averted, so as not to see the other's foreboding. 'It is too late.'

*

All the way to Keswick, Bea said, she kept fingering the envelope in her pocket, running her forefinger up and down the hard edge of it. Like it was the only certain thing to give her courage; that and the regular sharp sound of her boots on the gravel road, tsk-tsk-tsk. Sometimes it seemed to go on before her and other times to follow after and though the sound went on, the countryside seemed to pass so slow. An hour must have gone by and still Keswick was no more than a blur of grey roofs at the end of the lake. And all the time she had an ear cocked to the silence round her that was never quite silence; listening for the low buzz, the rise and fall like an eager growling sound of a car engine. Of course there were other cars in Keswick and other people that drove on the back roads. But Bea could only think that it would be him.

It rained a bit, she said, thin cold rain drifting over the hillsides and through the valley, making everything dark as it passed. And you could watch it pass, like it was a real thing, holding a shape. Like a huge grey ghost, she said, making you shiver.

She got past the first big house, walking between the tall beech hedges that grew either side of the road, the outskirts of Keswick so close she was almost upon them, almost within their safety, when she heard the car. She heard him change gears for the bend behind her, the roaring dropping away and then bursting out again. It stopped her dead in her tracks. And then she was helter-skelter over the gravel, like a scared rabbit, first to one side and then the other. But there was nowhere she could hide. She thought of crouching in the ditch, but he would only see her and then what could she say. If she could hide her face, she thought, p'raps he wouldn't see it was her. And she bent quickly, fumbling at the laces of her boots. She didn't notice the envelope fall out of her pocket with the jerky movement, she didn't hear the soft clatter of it on the gravel. But he did. He screeched to a stop.

'Hey,' he called, 'you've dropped something.'

There wasn't anything else she could do then, but look up. And there he was, one arm over the back of the passenger-seat and a sneer on his face like he'd known where to find her all along.

'Running away?' he drawled. And then so low and quick Bea hardly made out the words except by the menace in his voice. 'Bring that here.'

She didn't move; said she couldn't, couldn't even turn her eyes to look where the letter lay. Just kept staring at him. But the click of the car door jolted her awake. She'd already scooped up the envelope and got it half-way into her pocket when he lunged for it.

'It's mine,' she whispered, no breath left in her body.

'No,' he snarled close in her face as he forced her fingers open and held the envelope up so Miss Camille's writing was plain to both of them, 'it isn't.'

'I'm posting it. In Keswick.'

'I'll do that.' He swung himself back into the narrow car seat, jaunty as anything now. 'You can tell your mistress it's all been taken care of.'

Miss Camille was standing at the side window of the drawing room when Bea got back, worn out and dishevelled, just before lunch.

'Miss . . .' she croaked from the door, but Miss Camille heard her.

'Oh, Bea . . .' she said with a sad smile, advancing across the room. 'Bea, I am sorry.'

'Miss, I . . .' Bea lifted her hands and let them drop again.

'He caught you up, didn't he? It's all my fault, over-reacting. I should have given it to him to post in the first place. Just my brother!' She laughed, a high-pitched, strangled laugh and took Bea's hands, shaking them as if to make her laugh too. 'He knew you were gone, straight away; knew something was different. Ferreted about asking this and that. Soon as he heard you'd changed your day off, he was off out in that car like a whirlwind. He – he gets terribly jealous, thinks all sorts of silly things. You do understand, don't you, Bea? And I'm sorry for the upset you must have had. And all that walk – for nothing.' And she laughed again.

There was dark all round her eyes, Bea said, and she'd never held her hands before, never so much as touched her; she wasn't the familiar sort, Miss Camille. Bea just nodded and bit at the inside of her lip.

'And – and we'll probably be going back to London at the end of the month.' She turned away to her window again, running her hands over the backs of chairs. 'Weather's so poor this summer,' she murmured.

Bea heard the real story in the kitchen. It had started with shouting that blew up like a tornado that they couldn't help but hold open the kitchen door to hear; Mr Brookes getting beside himself. And doors banging. And running upstairs, her first and then him and more doors banging. And sobbing. They couldn't make out what started it. And then Mr Brookes comes flouncing into the kitchen, no nice manners any more, a sharp, mean look on his face and his voice different – a thin snarl in it and the beginnings and ends of words missing. Where was Bea, he wanted to know. And why had she changed her day off? And menacing them, coming up close to them when they couldn't answer. Mrs Pikes had picked up her rolling pin and he'd backed off then. Such a fuss about a maid's day off! They couldn't work it out. And then they saw. He must've thought he'd been found out. He must've thought the mistress had sent Bea off with notes or whatever to the local solicitor, or even the police.

She did, Bea told them. And they gasped at her. To her brother.

'He knew something was up,' they said, shaking their heads. 'He was nervous as a kitten and dangerous as a cornered snake. He'd no sooner left us alone when she came in, pale as death. We saw him hovering behind the service door to listen. And she gave us notice. End of the month, she said. Going back to London. Well, we knew it was all up for him then.'

The cliffs rise high at Tintagel. And the little white-washed houses huddle in a long scatter above the bay.

'Oh, isn't it pretty!' exclaims Nan peering from the windows of the coach.

'Yes,' says Moira, watching her closely, not looking at the houses or the street or the church or the old place they called the Post Office. 'Yes,' she murmurs. ''Tis.'

The bus inches along the narrow high street, but Moira, staring out of the window, sees only Jeth, standing by his old grey car under the elms at Sladdacoombe, waiting for her. Not waiting for Nan.

'Jeth's coming down to pick me up from the village,' Nan had said, squeezing herself, breathless, into the coach seat beside Moira, 'I told him I'd be dead beat after the day out.'

But there'll be no Nan. Only her. Moira clutches the handle of her black leatherette shopping bag tighter till her nails dig into the palm of her hand. Only her. Walking stately as a queen down the coach steps, over the gravelled road. Jeth opening the car door for her, smiling; in front of all the village. And then away they'll drive. Not to the farm, not to Davy's long face, but away . . . Away over the hills. The car just a little black dot.

'Here we are,' says Nan brightly.

The driver was standing up.

'Four o'clock, ladies. Four o'clock sharp just round about here. Can't miss me – I'm too big! Four o'clock, now, and we won't wait for any stragglers.'

Back into the cardboard world, with its cardboard smiles and mouthed phrases and its slow hours to be ticked by, while the real world pounds and flares inside her and leaps with such shrieking sometimes, she's sure the others must hear it. But they're all too busy getting down out of the bus, a slow, intent waddle of well-padded behinds.

'Merlin's Tea-rooms.'

'Well!'

It's a real sea day, blue and warm with a blustery, teasing wind that blows their skirts up and tugs at their hair.

Inside the café there's a long table ready for them. Moira has to push to make sure she sits next to Nan. First it's a relief to be sitting down out of the wind. Then it's warm. Then it's close. Condensation running down the small, crowded windows, all the tables full and the waitresses flustered. Moira smiles. She couldn't have arranged it better herself.

'Hot, isn't it?' she prompts.

'Close,' agrees Nan and begins unbuttoning her cardigan.

'Well now, ladies?' asks the waitress.

'We're having the two-course lunch,' says Mrs Ray, the outing organiser.

'Plaice 'n chips, pasty 'n chips, or cold chicken salad.'

'Oh!' Mrs Ray's mouth turns down. 'What's the other course?'

'Fruit pie 'n custard.'

'I'm having the plaice,' says Moira firmly. 'You going to have the fish, Nan? Always have fish at the sea,' she adds loudly and smiles at Mrs Matt and Mrs Treglowan who turn briefly to look at her. 'Always so fresh, isn't it?'

'Thought I might have the chicken,' says Nan in a low voice.'

'Oh no,' whispers Moira in a hissing of breath, 'you don't want to do that. Could be stale; kept. Could be

167

leftovers, from someone's plate! All messed up in mayonnaise you can't tell. And as for pasty, that's always leftovers.'

'Fish and I don't always agree . . .'

Moira smiles indulgently, the smile wrapping itself slowly over her face. Where had she first heard Nan say that – Tremorne, Brinksome? Never forgotten it. Always the same silly phrase.

'. . . but p'raps just this once . . .'

Mrs Treglowan and Mrs Matt stare sympathetically at her.

*

Miss Camille ate lunch alone. May took it in to her. Bea didn't like it, giving over her cap and apron, but she couldn't argue.

'She said it would be best if you had the rest of the day off, since that's what's been said,' May told her coming back with Miss Camille's empty soup plate.

'Best that way, our Bea; keep out of his sight for today.'

She ate with Mrs Pikes at the kitchen table. Leftovers from the dining room the night before, fried up. But she felt too agitated to do more than pick at them. May kept coming in and out with the tray; empty dishes and the new course. Bea's starched cap and apron coming in and out, in and out and Bea not in them. May clattered the dirty plates onto the draining board with a tight, buttoned-up smirk on her face. And it was all Bea could do not to leap up and grab the tray from her. She didn't know how to look after Miss Camille. She wouldn't do it right. Miss Camille liked things quiet and nice; genteel. When May was gone out again then it was worse. The kitchen silent, drawn back into its corners. Over everything there was a smell of frying and bones simmering on the back of the range and the thin, piercing odour of carbolic underneath it all. Across the table Mrs Pikes shovelled food into her mouth, complaining all the time about the notice she and May had been given and where, almost at the end of the season, was she going to find another position? But how, if she did and was required immediately, she would go, just like that, never mind no end-of-the-month. Bits fell out of Mrs Pikes's mouth as she talked and were pounced on and squashed quickly by her fork and pushed back in again. Bea's eyes never left Mrs Pikes's face, but she scarcely heard what the rapidly moving mouth said. She was listening. For the car. She kept hearing it. The way he'd revved up for the corner and changed down again to burst upon her. Over and over. Only she knew it wasn't real.

The sun came out and the wind chased it away again with clouds.

Mrs Pikes made her take a chair and sit outside in the warm corner between the rain butt and the back door. She found herself staring at the white undersides of ferns and grasses blown in one undulating wave after another up the hill. An endless ripple of white and green, like water, rushing upwards. It seemed like hours she gazed at it, lost in it. Just like Miss Camille. Sitting. Waiting. For him. But everything changed. Everything somehow – over. The day flattened and empty; and the house silent.

When they were all gone, Bea thought, and the house fallen in, the wind and the grass would go rippling up the hill just the same.

Mrs Pikes called her in just before five for a cup of tea. She took her chair and shut the door, glad suddenly to sit by the range. And still he hadn't returned.

*

It was cold and grey and neither land nor sky seemed separated one from the other when we set out from La Pianta. There was no celebration. No excitement. No pride in our taking to horse, all in a fidgeting line between the silent ranks of fellow-servants grouped to bid farewell to His Grace the Duke. Not like two days before when the others left with the baggage. That was a carnival setting out, such laughing and foolery from those on horseback and those that watched them go. We were more like a wake. In silence we watched the Duchess to her carriage, her women left behind red-eyed and weeping as if they would never see her again, and those to go with her pale and nervous, fussing with fur rugs and stone bottles of heated water. The company went so still that the whisper of her pointed slippers could be heard on the stone steps, so silent that the wings of a raven flying overhead creaked loud and its hoarse cry floated over us like a jeering laugh. She paused for a moment at the step of the coach, silence to silence as she looked at them and they at her, staring as though at some distant object already set apart, already taken from them. Only the Duke did not turn his head to see her.

Filippo was brought out last, between two of the Duke's bodyguards and set on a horse attached by a leading rein to the saddle of one of them, as if he was a prisoner. There was a murmur then ran through the groups of watchers. But the Duke drowned it out quickly, spurring his horse forward so that we were all pulled after him as if our horses were pricked by invisible lances.

No sooner had La Pianta sunk into the land behind us than a thick fog surrounded us, keeping us prisoner ourselves, all the way to Chioggia. The silence of it preyed on us, the muffled, held stillness. Beneath its softness there came a chill, a dankness that pierced us to the bone. An army could have lain in wait to ambush us and we would not have seen it. We could make out only the trodden roadway before us, the edges of the black fields running away into whiteness and the dark lines of sedge marking the channels and ditches beside us, warning us of their danger. We glanced back often at the black shape of the Duchess's coach swaying over the rutted road behind us, alone, with no outrider to protect her. Tomaso caught our glances and our muttering.

'Single file,' he snapped over his shoulder and we dropped back into uneasy silence.

Hour after hour and only the creak of the Duchess's carriage and the quick clicking of horses' hooves as they bunched and fell back again, uneasy as ourselves at this white, cold thing that pressed around us. Even the ring of our bridles had a false sound, a jarring, jangling note.

Yet as we neared Chioggia and the sluice beside us widened into a canal and small houses appeared each with its vine arbour no more than dried, twisted sticks, so the fog began to dissolve and our spirits, tentatively, to lift. We entered Chioggia's main street, the canal beside us ornate now with houses and bridges and churches, and all around us the crowds bowed and swept off their caps, for the Duke was master here, too. At Chioggia's end the street widened into a great piazza which gave onto the lagoon. The water was cold-looking like iron with short choppy waves that ran up to the stone buttresses and foamed over the lip of the patterned marble floor. We reined in our horses, already dancing and skittering at the sight of the water stretching like a treacherous road before them, and slid numbly from our saddles. A black barge with waiting oarsmen heaved at the water's edge. We saw Filippo led towards it.

'Soup and wine in the inn behind you.' Tomaso hurried past us. 'We leave in one hour.'

We stared at him, alarm tightening our faces.

'Do we not board ship?'

'The afternoon advances – it is already past . . .'

'The Duke will *dine*!' Tomaso searched our faces to discover which one of us was the malefactor.

But the Duke ate nothing. Meat was, indeed, laid out for him, but we saw him toy only with some bread. He sat at the back of the inn room with a fire of his own, glancing now and then at an hourglass he had on the table in a silver case, and staring into the fire. We stood

uneasily together near the door and all we talked of was
our journey and all we looked at was the Duke.

'We will not make Venice before dark.'

'We cannot even make Alberoni, now, before the sun
sets!'

'What of the Duchess?' someone murmured after a
pause.

We had seen her women come in to beg for hot water,
eyes lowered and cheeks flushed to enter such a rough
den of strangers. We had thought of the young Duchess
forced to wait outside in her carriage in the cold. But
none of us dared answer.

When we took ship at last, the sky had darkened as
though with snow or rain and a black wind came from
the sea cutting the grinning waves white that burst
against our sides with an icy slap; our ears sang with it,
our cheeks were numb with it, our eyes streamed and
wherever we turned our hunched shoulders we could find
no shelter from it. Out between the double line of black
poles marking the safe channel we went. Chioggia faded,
all its life – its domes and towers and tiled roofs – dwindled to a dark scribbling against the sky, gone from us.
We felt the oarsmen falter in the strong grip of currents
that seized us, snatched from them only when the wind
buffeted us. Pellestrina, little more than a smudged line
ahead, drew itself out along the horizon. No more than
a spit of land, a sand bar against the raging of the sea.

Within its lee shore we tore ourselves at last from the
grip of the tides, our mumbled praying drowned out by
the pounding of the surf on the seaward side of the island.
Above the dunes we saw the clouds part, at first in tiny
rents and slits of cream and rose and then in long,
streaming ribbons: apricot, green and flame.

*

Reed bending dark under a sharp wind and a wide, white
sky. Everything lined out clear: the winding of the Pont

St Honore track, the cuts where the reed parted now this way, now that and the high ridge of the dunes against the sky. Nothing hid. And every sound as clear and close to our ears as though the whole marsh had telescoped itself to fit under a glass jar. A day, as we used to say in those parts, under the eye of God.

All week we had been working our way along the silted-up channel from its beginnings close to the water meadows down towards the long pools that lay before the dunes and now we were come to its end. Come uncomfortably close to old Marsat's place. As we left the track and pushed in among the reed we felt ourselves under scrutiny, self-conscious and awkward, though the marsh seemed emptied of any other creature.

Later and later it got, though there was no sun visible to mark the passage of the morning, but no sound came from the house, no smoke from the chimney. Only the bickering of the ferrets and the rattle of links dropping against each other as the dog walked dejectedly out to the length of its chain and back again.

It had become their habit lately. As though they wished to prolong the pretence of sleep, or sleep itself. To postpone the waking again into battle, into tormentor and tormented.

No argument, no reason could pull Leon from his nightly watching at their window, though the danger now to him, since Jean-Luc was gone so wild, was greater than ever. So it was that we knew how Laurette strove to keep herself apart from him. She did not eat with him. She would not put her chair in the evenings within arm's reach of him. She had found a small oil lamp with a cracked globe, Leon had seen her cleaning the rust from it, and this she set up near the window on the upturned end of an old fish crate with her chair drawn next to it.

There she had sat the night before with her breviary in her lap almost hid in the folds of her dress, just her hands either side of it. Jean-Luc, at his usual place at the table, had sat glowering at her for some time, unravelling the end of a length of rough hempen twine that lay in a tangle of things before him. Leon saw how more and more he bent his attention to it, twisting the wiry filaments into long tassles and knotting their ends. Finally he leaned back, grinning, on two legs of his chair and reached towards the wooden shelf behind him. Leon saw the tips of his fingers close round a thin stick propped against the wall. Outside the window Leon drew back, but Laurette, it appeared, saw nothing. It was a long withy cane cut, no doubt, from one of the willows up near St Honore. His mouth half open, his shoulders hunched as if he drew into himself with glee, Jean-Luc tied the twine to one end of the stick. And then he swivelled round in his chair to face his wife. She lifted her hand to turn the page. Out flicked the whip so fast Leon scarcely saw him move, but he heard Laurette's gasp and saw her hand fly up from the book as if it had been burned. Jean-Luc leaned back against the table, his lop-sided grin hung on his open mouth and his eyelids drooped over his eyes hiding their gleam. The stick lay still across his knees, the knotted strings hanging down between his legs. An uneasy stillness fell between husband and wife, a tentative watching stillness. Laurette took the page of the missal between finger and thumb again and lifted them. The whip flashed out again and, as he saw the thin page tear, Leon heard her cry out. She tried to push the page over with the hand farthest away from him, but again the whip lashed down over her fingers so that she leaped in her chair. Each time she touched the page the lash of the whip was there almost before her as if he read her very thoughts, so that she had no place left in which to hide from him.

She bent her head to read the same words over, since he would not have her turn the page, and the knotted strings slashed at her face. A sob burst out of her and her hands clapped themselves to her eyes.

'You mind you give your attention to me. Come here!'

She did not move.

'Come here!' he roared, lifting his arm and making the whip sing round her legs, over and over.

Hunched she sat and still as a stone. He leaped to his feet. And so, finally, did she. Then there began such a dance, such a darting to this side and that, such a stumbling forward and a twisting back out of the whip's path. Even when Leon could bear no more and turned away his head he could not keep out the sound of the lash hissing through the air and the staccato rhythm of her boots against the bare floorboard, her screaming that climbed higher and higher and under it all the sure, compact thud of the whip against her body, over and over, relentless.

He let her go. Or she escaped him. For the sound of the whip ceased and there was only sobbing echoing from somewhere closed in. Leon's first thought was that he had shut her in a cupboard. But over the sobbing came a scrabbling, scrambling sound, a blundering, lurching noise that grew steadily fainter. Leon uncovered his eyes – onto an empty, darkened room. He felt the autumn chill and the sweat cold on his back and the tenseness of the silence over the marsh.

And then, from one of the upper rooms, rang out a new scream.

Six twenty-five Mr Brookes returned. Bea heard the car
and looked up, straight into the face of the kitchen clock.
She heard the front door bang and steps down the hall
and she held her breath. But they weren't coming to the
kitchen, they faded away. They stood there, though, Mrs
Pikes and May and Bea, like they'd been turned to stone.
Listening. And then the drawing room bell started
twitching and shrilling on its wire.

'May, quick!' said Mrs Pikes.

'It's drinks,' said Bea, leaping up. 'Ice and nuts and . . .'

'Bea, sit down. Go on, May, go and see.'

'She hasn't changed,' muttered Bea under her breath.
She'd wanted to go to her, like an uneasy feeling, all
afternoon; now, Bea said, it was overwhelming. Miss
Camille had never not changed. Her fingers twisted
round each other, they picked things up from the kitchen
table – an onion, a fork, scrubbed carrots laid out in a
line – turning them over and over.

May burst through the service door.

'Lemon-on-a-plate-with-a-knife and ice-in-a-bowl and
them frilly . . .'

'May! She hasn't changed, has she, Miss Camille . .?'

'Nan, where's Nan? And that Moira Thompson? Where
they got to? We been all through Tintagel one side and
back the other!'

'Mrs Rudd saw them some time back outside a cake
shop.'

'What they want with cake so soon after lunch?'

'Well, p'raps they were hungry. They had that fish that Moira Thompson kept saying was off, remember?'

'They gone down the hill.'

'Down the hill?'

'They gone to see the castle, most like and Merlin's Cave.'

'Down that steep path, in all those rocks!'

There was a track from the jetty at Pellestrina to the far end of the island with sand blown over it so deep in places from the dunes on our right that the wheels of our carriages were caught frequently. We ploughed and lurched and slowed almost to stopping point as though invisible hands plucked at us, stopping us, holding us back. The light flared along the horizon, a gaudy play of colours, but we knew that even as they danced against the sky, darkness was closing swiftly in behind us.

The wind howled at the tattered hoods of the carriages and came in, icy fingered, through the many holes. It had torn the veil from the Duchess's face as she had stepped from the gilded cabin of the barge, sending it flying out over the water like a wraith, twisting and writhing and we had seen, even in the fading light, how pale she was. Yet none was pale as Filippo, huddled in a corner of our carriage, his eyes closed, his head turned away and his body shaking violently as if he was in a fever. None of us dared speak to him with Tomaso watching us, eagle-eyed. We sat, each with our own fear, in silence, till the dunes fell away and a low wall ran beside us, the glimmer of white stones – domes and crosses and shadowy figures – beyond it.

'Santa Maria del Mare,' whispered Bernardo.

And raggedly, one by one, we crossed ourselves.

The horses stopped and climbing out we saw a silent, reed-fringed bay before us, no habitation visible, no bird's cry, the water black and rippling at our feet and the light already dimmed. Across the dark water, Alberoni, on the next island, looked no more than a stone's throw away, lights flickering among the swaying trees that crowded it.

'Be gone!' Tomaso rapped sharply on the door of the nearest carriage and the coachmen, in a scrabble of sand and frightened, slithering hooves, turned their horses and lumbered away, leaving us to the wind and the frozen hiss of water against reed.

Only the sucking and gurgling of the water and our scythes falling heavy and out of rhythm. And all else silence.

'The fowl are gone,' I said at length, resting my scythe and gazing about me.

But Leon only jerked his head sideways and would not meet my eyes. We had heard no shooting on the marsh to scare them. Nor were there signs of storm. No unusual brilliance over the sea, or clouds gathering on the horizon. No sudden dropping of the wind. So we worked on, but we did no good to ourselves or the land.

Around mid-morning we saw Jean-Luc emerge from the house. We heard the porch door bang and we looked up. And bent our heads again quickly. We did not want to attract his attention, we did not want him near us. But we watched, nevertheless, from under caps, from below the bushiness of eyebrows to see him go. Up the path, between the reeds, his gun under his arm.

Perhaps she had been watching too, for it was then that she came hobbling out with her broom and began to sweep sand from the porch. Brushing away all track of him, it looked like. Brushing away all trace for a few hours, a few hours of grace. At the porch steps the dog wagged its tail and tried to lick her hand. And we saw how she instantly drew back from it with a jerky movement as though she could no longer trust the touch of any living thing. Guiltily, as if we, too, had laid a hand to her, we bent our heads again to our work.

Gone eight it was and still no bell for dinner. He was

up to his tricks again, Bea said, she knew it. She had twisted the dish cloth to string on her lap. And then it came, pealing out and dancing up and down like a jerky, dying thing high against the wall. Bea jumped up. But it was May she had to let take the soup in.

'Why don't you go to your room, Bea?' said Mrs Pikes.

Bea knew she meant it kindly, but she shook her head.

'I couldn't sit on my own,' she whispered.

When May came back into the kitchen with the empty plates she paused in front of Bea, leaning for a moment against the table.

'She's drunk,' she said, 'your Miss Camille.'

Bea felt her cheeks flush hot with the outrage.

'She's *never* drunk!' A hoarse whisper of breath all she could shout out across the table.

'She is now.' May clattered the plates down on the draining board. 'She's got a face on her I've never seen before, a real hard look. Knocked the pepper pot flying like she couldn't even see it.'

Couldn't see the town from down on the rocks where Moira finds them a nice sheltered spot out of the wind. Wind screaming and the roar of the sea so loud! Nan looks uneasy. The waves paw at the rocks so and everyone else seems to have gone, the people looking over the ruins with them.

'Time we got back isn't it, Moira?'

'Oh, we just got time for tea, Nan.'

'Tea?'

'Yes.' Moira pulls the mouth of the black shopping bag open. 'I brought it with me. Little thermos,' she sets it out, 'packet of crab sandwiches . . .'

'Oh, I couldn't touch crab, not after the fish at lunch.'

'No, well . . .' Moira smiles. 'Got some nice buttered fruit scones. Got them from that shop up in the High Street,' Moira jerks her head up at the steep cliff, 'made them butter them for me, that's what took so long. Remember?'

*

Down among the reed we crouched, our billhooks to one side of us. A cold wind had come up and the water, where we had freed it, ran grey as steel. Midday it felt like to our bellies, though we neither of us had the stomach to eat.

'Let us go back,' I said.

But Leon would not lift his head, he would not move, but stared miserably down at the water and the mud.

When Laurette came out again, he looked up sharp enough. Through the reed stems we watched her limp out to the pump at the side of the house. The ferrets screamed at her, clawing at the wire of their runs and the wind tore at her dress till it blew like rags. We saw her bend and strain at the stiff black handle, the creak of it a gasping, shrieking noise cut off in mid breath as the pail filled. We saw her stumble beneath the weight of it. We saw the water slop dark onto the sand and stain the porch steps. We heard the door slam itself behind her.

'We do no *good* here, Leon. Let us go!'

Suddenly all was speed, where before had been delay. Suddenly all was graciousness to the Duchess, where before she had been ignored. We saw her handed on the Duke's arm to the furthest gondola of the three waiting for us against the reeds. We saw her women packed in after her, the stone bottles and the rugs.

'Hurry, hurry!' Tomaso hissed at us, herding us along the shore. 'The five of you in the second boat.'

We crowded at the stern of our gondola, pushing at each other, shivering, stumbling one by one over the slatted seats. Our gondolier stood back in the darkness, but the Duchess's gondolier kept close to his boat, a small, eel-like man, more like a southerner, who stank worse than the others, a heavy, nauseous smell like rancid fat.

'After the next island,' we heard the Duchess say in

her high, clear voice to one of her women, 'we shall see Venice.'

And we felt, each of us, the sense of a net that had been loose about us, tighten suddenly.

Only the wind, rising and falling. Like a blade sharpening itself on a stone, icy-thin sound for a summer's day. And the gulls keening. Gulls always tell when there's food around. Perhaps they can see from high up Moira shuffling through her shopping bag. Perhaps, hovering overhead, they can see in the bag: the shaking fingers taking the bought scones out of a paper bag and putting home-made ones in their place.

'Never find anything in all this junk!' Moira pulls out the paper bag, tweaking it open, the bag that she's just twisted shut. 'Have a scone, Nan. And I'll pour the tea.'

Can't stop her fingers shaking. Can't stop the pictures playing in her head. Jeth standing by the open car door getting nearer and nearer. Doesn't hear the sea crash on Tintagel's rocks, only the dry scrunch of gravel beneath shoes.

There was no noise to fright him; I could not tell what alarmed him so. Yet he rocked there on his heels, backwards and forwards, his hands clapped over his ears, from time to time shaking his head. There was nothing. Nothing but that clear, unnatural silence over the marsh.

First there was silence, then there was noise and confusion. All at once, as if at a signal, our gondolier leaped on to the stern of our boat. From behind him in the gloom there was a muffled cry, a thud, the high-pitched scream of women, and men running on the bank – a swirl of dark, enveloping cloaks. The first gondola shot forward into the stream and we made out, in astonishment, the hunched figures of the Duke, Tomaso and the bodyguards. Our own boat lurched instantly after them so

that we scarcely had time to turn and see Filippo in the
stern of the Duchess's boat, sprawled as if he had been
thrown.

'Mr Brookes says we can go to bed soon as we've cleared
up. Soon as I've taken the coffee in to them. Says he'll
lock up.'

'No!' Bea pushed back her chair. 'No, we can't leave
her!'

'Now *then*, Bea.' Mrs Pikes turned on her. 'For goodness sake! You can't go to her now. You can't do nothing
for her.'

Can't take her eyes off Nan, off the scone in her lap. Off
her hand lying so near it.

Pick it up, Nan, she whispers in her head. Pick it up!

She must stretch out her hand too, she must take one
too, she must lift it . . . Nan's fingers close round the
scone. Hand to mouth. Lips part. Moira can't breathe,
can't move, can't watch. Never saw Lou – shut the door
fast. Ducks her head to stare at the grass, hand clenched
round her own scone, the safe scone.

Now, Nan, she shouts in her head. Now, bite!

My urging fell on deaf ears, my shaking of Leon's
shoulder could not stir him. Under my hand the sinews
of his back were tensed and strained all towards the
vision that he seemed to hold before his eyes as he gazed
down into the water. And then we heard the quivering
whine of the dog. We looked up, both of us. And there
she was standing in the doorway all dressed up in some
white-coloured fancy town dress with a shawl over her
shoulders. She let the door bang behind her and, leaning
heavily on the rail, levered herself down step by step
from the porch. We saw the pain of it clear, as if it now
affected her worse than before, or else she cared no longer
to conceal it.

182   *

She heard the jazz blare up loud, all of a sudden, and then die down again. Drawing-room door opening and closing, Bea thought to herself from where she sat, knees hugged to her chest, halfway up the back stairs where they gave onto the main landing. Then Miss Camille's step on the front stairs, only muffled and uneven like stumbling. And half a staircase length behind her, turning the lamps out one by one so that if she looked back she would see only darkness, *he* followed. And behind him, so she would think he was still downstairs, the jazz left to moan out with a sound like something shut up in a tin box. Up and up it climbed on notes that made Bea's hair stand on end and then fell, whimpering down, to a cringing whisper.

She had trouble opening her door, Bea could hear. Then came the hard drumming of water thudding against enamel – Miss Camille drawing her bath. And the urge to go to her, to do it for her; to lay out her towels and measure the mustard powder, to shut the door against draughts, against . . . But it was too late. Over the steam curling up in a soft beam of light thrown across the landing from the not-quite-shut door, a shadow passed. A dark shadow. And the door was closed, not shut – that could have made a noise – pulled to, so that the light was gone.

Like the dropping down of night around us, we knew then. God forgive us, we thought first of our own safety, reaching, each of us, surreptitiously under our cloaks to still our trembling fingers on the handles of our daggers.

There was a sudden glint of light on metal among the reeds near the track and we caught sight of Jean-Luc crouched down, the stock of his gun resting against his shoulder, the barrel raised.

Up and back. Up and back over the flowered print of Nan's dress goes the shadow of her arm. Moira can't hold the scone any more, can't bear the silence any more, only the pounding of the waves and the licking hiss of spray, white tongues foaming over the rocks. She should give Nan tea, make her wash it down. Make her . . . Hand shaking so she can hardly grasp the thermos cup; the cup hot, burning. She holds it out.

On out into the stream, the lagoon opening to one side of us and the last colours softening to jade and cream all along the dark rim of the mainland. The island before us black and we caught in a lake of silver. The exertions of our gondolier now a harsh whispering roar like words not understood and we jolted at every stroke of his pole, the breath tight in our bodies, staring back, beyond him into the dusk. We saw her boat at last nose out into the reeds; we saw figures, dark shapes against the sky. But the gasp of relief that we let out at the sight caught again in our throats. Why was it that her boat came on so slow?

From tuft to tuft of marram grass she hauled herself, the sand sliding treacherous around her, the shawl, clutched in one hand, streaming out behind her like a flag. And all the while the whine of the dog winding in the beating of our hearts tighter and tighter till wind and sea were drowned out.

All there was now was sound. Bea sat on the back stairs, hands pressed over her ears, but the tighter she pressed the more she heard – like she was forced to listen. Miss Camille wouldn't have heard him come, not over the welling and pounding of the water. But the pounding stopped and then, like Miss Camille was putting her foot through delicate muslin or silk and tearing it gently, she heard her step into the bath, the water parting for her: once, twice. And then the wave-like swoosh of her sitting down, the water going up and down from end to end of the bath, the swell getting smaller and smaller, settling itself. And that funny squeaky sound, like a rude noise, people always made as they slid down, their skin against the bath, as they found a comfortable position and stretched out.

In under the shadow of the land we came, and out into the dropping light she followed, the gulf between us widening. Black water and silver water out in the central channel where the tide ripped and tumbled. We felt it tug at our gondola but shot free of it and, looking round, saw the Duke already ashore. And then we heard . . .

Always silence after the squeaky sound – silence of pleasure and rest.

. . . she reached the ridge of the dune and stood there unsteadily, sleeves billowing, gathering in her . . .

. . . only in there it wasn't silent. There was a flurry and a gasp and something wooden kicked.

Nan's arm jerks out, knocks the cup to the ground. Spray of tea, spray of crumbs, high-pitched choking scream . . .

. . . scream against scream, cutting the darkness like knives, blade against blade . . .

. . . like a twig snapped over our heads, like the dry hard crack of a lightning bolt, a shot rang out. Then another . . .

. . . threshing, knocking sound like the back legs of a pinioned rabbit, and waves slapping at the sides of the path . . . Nan hooped like a bow snapping. Arched and curled and . . . up on the dune ridge arms flung . . . flung against the sky as the boat sank under them, a tangle of dark shapes . . . She balanced a second longer; she half-turned to the sea. Then down she came . . . Down, inch by inch, something being pushed down, like a stone down a slate, squeaking. Inch by inch, shrieking, clinging . . . running or falling we could not tell, slithering in the soft sand . . . Moira screams and jumps up – not Nan now this howling, writhing thing. Runs to the path. 'Help!' she cries . . . 'Help, ho!' strong over the water on the icy wind. Filippo. Strong. Then cut off in a gurgling shriek, in a glotting of sound . . . waves booming all the length of Belle Plage . . . waves slopping up over the top of the bath and splashing on the floor, over and over . . . over the sand and up the porch steps she dragged herself . . . down into the tide race of the Porto di Malamocco, only a dark, roiling tangle of heads and arms, only fingers jerking like sticks in a river . . . hands claw at herself, clawing a hole, a breach for the burning tide to spill out . . . water at her neck, over her chin, legs kicking fainter at the bath's sides . . . sky reeling and the earth sliding away . . . looped and curled and tearing at the ground with her nails, neck taut with the pain . . . hands tearing at his hands, stifling her gasping screams; bites at his fingers – bites water . . . water-logged arms flailing, heavier and heavier . . . down she sank on the porch, the bright sky gone dark to her eyes . . . the world slipping . . . hair floated loose, dark mass like seaweed and then gone . . . lower she slides, blur of known things – taps winking – fading . . . scream twisted to hoarse breath in her throat, jerking slower and slower . . . breath a sob . . . water closing over her head as her fur cloak dragged her down . . . held her down, held her fast . . . sea roaring under her head, up through the earth . . . waves pounding . . . water roaring . . . roaring in her head . . . roaring in her ears . . . hand scrabbling in grass . . . against the insubstantiality of water . . . of air . . . tightening on his . . . nails . . . jerked . . . and was still.

MAGGIE HEMINGWAY
THE POSTMEN'S HOUSE

Escaping to England from a Czechoslovakia still locked
behind the Iron Curtain, Jan finds a job as a postman.
Longing to belong in the land of his dreams, he learns the
rules and hierarchy of the Postmen's House – and tastes
its power. But his wife Eliska, haunted by memories of
her life in Prague, cannot forget the past. The gulf in their
perspectives on freedom widens until suddenly, and with
heart-rending consequences, the magic of England
dissipates.

'Her best novel . . . as if Graham Swift had written MRS
DALLOWAY'
Christopher Hawtree in The Spectator

'Written with remarkable imaginative power . . . a strong and
original novel'
Miranda Seymour in the Evening Standard

'Eliska's story is one of the heart, and utterly compelling'
Sally Edworthy in The Times

'An exciting novel, deeply felt and brimming with a passion
barely controlled'
Ruth Rendell in The Daily Telegraph

'A beautifully written and absorbing novel which explores
love, loss and freedom'
Today